THE BURNING PYRE

THE BURNING PYRE

DEVENDRA PUNSE

PARTRIDGE

ISBN: Hardcover   978-1-4828-8658-0
             Softcover   978-1-4828-8638-2
             eBook   978-1-4828-8639-9

Print information available on the last page.

To order additional copies of this book, contact
Partridge India
000 800 10062 62
orders.india@partridgepublishing.com

www.partridgepublishing.com/india

Mother, thou art a child of earth and sky.
Limitless is thy love and care!
Mother, thou art a lady with nature shy.
Kind is thy heart and face fair.

----- To my mother -----

With a loud screech, the overcrowded
bus halted at the bus station.
I stumbled away, holding my aching head with
my right hand, to near the bus station.
I glanced up at the cloud-smitten sky,
then down the way to walk safely.
A long travel of 150 km made my nerves
tremble, and it seemed that I was fainting.

The passengers gave me a dashing gush behind and I trembled at a thought of having to lick the mud. The heavy crowd of people was swarming all around carelessly. Crazy crowd; crowd colourless and careworn! Nobody craved for a mood to wait even for a minute. The crowd spiced up the life of this land. And people breathed down their land's neck. The heavy crowd blocked my way. Crossing the watery ditches and saving my plastic-coated tiny bag from pouring raindrops, I entered into the bus station anyhow. I anticipated a little place to sit in, but the reign of heavy crowd turned down my anticipation. I cursed under my breath for not adjusting a seating place and thought myself a poor soul. I spent a moment or two in aiming a move. I noted with some self-contempt that my exit from home was inexcusable and punishment might draw on. I didn't think I was wise to be paraphrasing my mother's dumb approval for leaving home decidedly. Like most negligent men who deliberately neglected their duties, I had also flung my duty and escaped home.

I smiled to myself.

Ganesh Chaturthi was just over, and
Dussera was drawing to a close.
It was Ghatasthapana Day.
TUESDAY
Unseasonable rain turned into a heavy shower.
All three months of monsoon season went
dry despite a few late spells of rain.
Scanty rain had instilled a worrisome
terror in the farmers' mind.

Never was the feeling of exertion so strong, I felt. Grey and gloomy thoughts fell on my soul like a heavy windstorm. A sharp rapping sound and the cries of people shook the whole surrounding. The last night was terrific! Although it had been raining cats and dogs, I had passed the night like a hardened sinner. A melancholic condition in home was quite difficult to keep up the fight against. Even the seconds were passed on beyond endurance. A thousand sad thoughts had been flowing through my head like the waves dashing to the shore. What most awful was that the event was so clear and tearful to subdue. Sinfully expensive event!

Reproaching myself for my life, I astonished at even those nearest ones as to why they all behaved heavily with my family. I knew my agonies well for I loved them more than my dear ones. As clock strikes second, minute, hour, my heart throbs agony. It was difficult for me to bear deadly sad and unlucky occurrence that could delve into the living heart. Love, linear attraction, one flesh, remained the most important screw in family life; father and mother being the two pillars? Two hands of the watch! Two unified souls! Two inseparable entities! Minus one might be a great, great damage!

I had a very tearful, sad night and had passed it seating beside my mother. In the morning, with terrific efforts, I made up my mind to leave the home. Heavily, more heavily than ever, rain started its dance. Bandaging all my courage, determination, crisis, hypnotically I had crossed the door of the home, leaving my grief-stricken mother and two sisters at their own risk. How very ugly, unruly that was! A great sinner am I? Wished I was mistaken in such condition! I felt I wanted that scene out my sight for achieving my goal, my duty, but it was peculiarly horrible to think that an only son had been out of home lapsed into impatience. A tinge of cruelty in my singularity could be seen overtly. My mother's permission was amazing! Speechless she had beckoned and the tears welled up to her eyes. I thought myself a rotten bounder.

I stood near a bench pressing the file close to my chest (*my important certificates and documents inside*). Uneasiness made me restless and unruly. Crowd and crowd of terrible thoughts were throttling me. The old clock on the wall of the bus station was warning to strike ten thirty. My wristwatch was silent like a dumb man. It needed repair. Rain damaged it. Did I really need a wristwatch? Simply it is a time machine, nonetheless I could say! Silent! Might be hushed up like my fate! Oh, no! Fate is a scary, dirty word!

I had to kill time till one o'clock. I could manage myself to reach the college (*my destination where I had to attend an interview*) within half an hour, even if I started from here at twelve o'clock exactly. I tried to get the place to sit in but found no vacant place. Not a single bench was vacant. Place? The biggest problem here? My god! No place to sit in; no place to live in. *This city has ten million souls/some are living in the mansions/some are living in the holes/But there is no place to live in, my dear, there is no place to live in*—sang a poet in his beautiful poem. Recollection of the lines dashed me into a pathetic thinking. True. Exclusively true. In school days, one question was invariably asked in compulsory English paper on the topic '*A Scene at a Railway Station*' or '*A Scene at a Bus Station*' which was a terrific topic for me to write even a single line for shorting minute observation and never could I write a good essay on those topics. Minute observation of anything became my habit today. This changing scenario of the present lifestyle—terrible! Change occurred everywhere! Travel? Numberless buses. Complete motorisation. Rash driving. Arrogant attitude. Snobbish behaviour. Huge crowd. Countless people. And resulted accidents. Murders, robberies, rapes, kidnapping, attacks, agitations, strikes, and suicides—growing everything. But—existence? Man's existence? Where should a man seek an existence? Where should a man see his face safer? Where should a man live in peace? And the next, why should a man seek an existence? Sybaritic attitude made the modern man a slave to an easy life. Man became man's biggest foe. Sensibility declined at throes! Chaos?

Close to me on a bench, one old man was busy in reading the newspaper. But he was feigning really! In fact, he was closely observing the girl who was seated closer to him. Fashionable she looked but swanky. A small child of around 3 or 4 years, richly dressed, was busy in eating Dairy Milk Silk very consciously, sitting at her feet on the dirty floor. Dairy Milk Silk—about sixty to sixty-five rupees price! Rich child indeed! Dared not say a spoilt brat! She took out a bottle of water of her bag and drinking water heavily, said harshly to that old man, 'Hey, old man—crawl a little—give me some place?' and carried her son up on the bench by other hand. The old man, reluctantly, spaced and tried himself to immerse into reading. At a moment, my eyes captured the news on the front page of the newspaper heading—'Two more farmers commit suicides in Yavatmal District.' As soon as the heading of the news bruised my eyes, I tried to read the news impatiently. But, lo! That old man scrolled the paper and scowled at me. The worst of it was that he had no aptitude for reading. 'Gratis reading not allowed!' he might have barked.

Suicide!

Death! Unwilling death! Unwanted death!

Mid October.

Beginning of harvest season.

The farmers of this region are exhausted. And now the real battle for survival would start, and by giving up all hopes, the farmers would run away from the battlefield of life—would meekly submit to death. A soldier sacrifices his life for the cause of nation; a farmer destroys his life for merely the wants of life—quick as lightning, a thought leapt into my mind. It is urgent that the private sector investment has to pick up. Industry has to go beyond organising seminars. Public spending has increased, foreign investment has increased, and industry now has to do its bit. The efforts must be put in to develop agriculture sector. It is an urgent need of the hour.

Last year, I had presented a research paper in the National Conference organised by the economics department of one reputable college on *Suicides of Farmers in Vidarbha Region: Reasons and Remedies.* But had there been any useful or fruitful discussion on the topic? How many professors had discussed the problem? How many professors had asked the questions, had searched out the reasons, and had participated in the conference? Many of them hailed from the farmers' families, in fact? And still, all had dared no sensitivity to come on the front to discuss the realities and problems? Had it been the National Conference? Even the key speaker of the conference had been beating about the bush! He had scanty knowledge and study of farmers' problems. The chairman of the society had delivered his speech serving no purpose. And for others, the farmers' suicide was a useless subject. Such conferences must discuss the matter with full purpose. It should not go useless. Novices like me must seek an opportunity to participate in the event with full preparation. Healthy discussion must play the pivotal role at the root of organising the conferences. Is it my grudge?

Might be a true grudge?
Rain speeded up.
With bleak eyes, I still was observing
the humdrum of life.
Drowsiness hunted back. Sleeplessness
covered up. Anxiety hovered around.
I found no vacant bench. Standing at
the pillar, I flapped my eyes.
My mind again had a brief visit to home.
Devastated! All branded in pathos!
All thickened in sorrows!
All scattered. All smothered.
And even then, the only son of a family
was 150 km away from home.
How haughty and rude I am?

mother—mother's face troubling me—her wrinkled face blaming me—her deem eyes scolding me—n why not—right—she is right—mother—my mother—mother of—son n two daughters—working all day in n day out—in the field—earning for us—sweating hard—for bread n butter—her lean n lipid body—narrates—story of survival—sacrificing so much for family—second cause of sustenance—father—first—n son—only son—am

i her only son—what son meant to be then—can i
pay—price of her tears—can i pay—price of father's
trust—repair—loss—can i take—aggressive step
against—uncle's revengeful acts—uncle's deeds—
intolerable—what revenge he—taking against
father— childless father—patient of asthama
walking -- medicine shop—everything -- at his
disposal—*n* my father— grand worker—great
fighter of odds—kind man—simple—burdened
under—family responsibilities—adjusting
money—wryly—anyhow—for education—for
cultivation—illness—but—courageously fighting
out—problems—like—great warrior—father—
thou art— shield—*n*—shield—

MOTHER MOTHER MOTHER

*He came in the house like a narcissistic bull
shouting, ''ll kill,'ll kill, stop—a while!' and in a sudden
move retrogressed and sat on the ground and began
swirling the ends of his broad moustache and brushing
his goatee beard. He was behaving like a vehement,
vindictive Greek god. Knowing not anything of his
mood, I stood before him and looked ignorantly, but
he changed his mood and gave a resounding slap on
my right cheek and even bit me like an animal. Crying
harshly again ''ll kill you, 'll kill' he rose up and broke
the long wooden stick hard pressing on his bony thigh.
'You, swine! Don't come near—'wise 'll kill you, go,
go, don't come near—?' Wild madness made him mad.*

Seeing me alone at home, he again became very brutal and abused my father in bedraggled words. 'Harra-a-a-m-khor—tries to capture my land—my land!—mine!—see you?' and spread his angered look at every nook and corner of the house. Seeing nobody in the house, again he took me into task severely. I was beyond the age of understanding of that much serious matter. But something was very serious? He waited for a moment and then hissing like a cobra went out.

Waiting for mother prolonged that day for further two hours. Under the scorching sun, the mother entered home, tired, beleaguered, puckish, sheepish, she wiped out sweat from her face and drank glass after glass of water, relaxed for a while and looking very pitifully at the cradle in which my small sister had slept, said to me, 'Had a meal?' and cleaned the rolling tears by the corner of a lugada, but she could not control her tears. She wept. She went near to the cradle, and uncovering the face of her small kid, she bent down and kissed her cheeks. She writhed around on the floor in agony. It disturbed me and lovingly I asked her, 'What happened—maa?' She could not accommodate even a word to utter, but cornered her face smoothly. Spookiest happening was ahead? And her cadaverous and stooped body made it clear that she was suffering from a severe pain. Crisscross of agonised lines blackened her face like a rain-loaded cloud.

My mother, a priceless treasure for me, fainted and gasped. Her chest throbbed like a blacksmith's bellows. Her agonised body and closed eyes made me so fearful and confused that I could not understand the situation. I sat at her head and put my hand on her forehead. She shivered with pain and temperature and blurred some words. I put my hand on her chest and asked, 'Mother, mother what happened?' She was numb. I ran out of the home to call someone for the help. 'Help! Help!' I cried, but nobody came in sight. Day was up. Heat was at the peak. Fearfully, I cried for father, who had yet to reach home back from the field.

I rushed back home and again
sat at the mother's head.
There sounded the fearful titter—tit!
titter—tit! titterrr—of the peewit.

My little heart palpitated fast. Fear seized me. I was the only saviour of my mother at that time at home. Suddenly, like a whirlwind, he appeared again roaring, 'Where is that bloody bastard? Won't—I won't leave him today? My revengeful mind is rock solid today. I won't—'ll him!" He waggled in fury and entered the place where my mother was lying calmly. I stood up. Some divine spirit and strength infused in me and I went near him and cried, 'Go back.' He caught me in the clutches and gave a resounding slap on my right cheek again. Uncontrolled, I fell on the ground. It was a severe blow for the boy of 9 years. 'Where is your father? That coarse pig?' he tethered his teeth in extreme jealousy, pride, and fury. I rose up from the ground and in a severe gush of anger gave him a quick blow with my ablest vigour. But I was too small to fight with that strong man. He slapped me hard in return and roared, 'Abey, you trifle gnat—'ll die uselessly. Get off with just a warning, I tell you! Want your father? And what happened to this witch? Noutanki! She is a real planner! She is a real conspirator! Way off—way off—hey, you don't feign—witch—you're a real witch—you play with my wife—you play all this game—troubles my wife—my children—you're a real troublemaker—get up—get up—get up' and plucked my mother's hand. I gave again a severe blow to him and tried to pull him away from her. He pushed me back with his strong elbow. My stomach crumpled with pain. I fell down and cried, 'Maa! Maa!'

   When my father came back home, I narrated the happening furtively, but my father realised the situation, and in an utter fury roared like a lion, 'Where is that bastard? It's all over now? Comes upon my family? Come, come, come quickly, out you rascal?' I saw my father's raged face for the first time. He stormed out of the home in a rage calling that bastard uncle. That bastard lived in an adjoining house, but before my father would catch him, he ran away stealthily and surprisingly nobody found at his home. I tried to calm my father but he was quite uncontrollable. He threw a stick in the corner and sat on the floor, gasping and coughing. I offered him a glass of water. He drank water and went to mother's bed. Testing a palm on mother's forehead, and feeling her pulse, he asked, 'How are you?' Mother couldn't speak. She felt a warm of husband's palm and tears deceived her. Clearing tears from her weakened eyes, he said, 'Don't care until I'm here? I'm alone *able to fight out all odds—remember? He'll definitely get punishment for his brutal deed. I've done a lot for him—never cared for self and family. I tried to give him whatever he demanded since the death of my father and mother. Wasting money on his three marriages, I wholeheartedly tried to bring his life on the shore. Did hard work and saved him from many corruptive deeds and even from misappropriation case—saved him from imprisonment. Spared nothing to protect him and the same man—who called himself my younger brother— revolted against me—tried to harm my wife—bit my son—won't leave him—no, I won't leave him?'*

No sooner did he finish his ambulatory words than my mother, severely writhing in pain, looked at my father's convulsed face and appealingly said, 'No, no, don't do this. That man is mad. A brute indeed! But very cunning too! Any revengeful deed is very common for him. Save us from him, but without any quarrel, without any physical violence. That's the only safest way for us? Look at these small children. Look at my condition. Look at yourself. No, this is a bad time on us. Don't go by his way? He is a childless man, and never cares for his third wife—don't add to the more pangs and pain—it will be unmindful riding on furious chariot—' she gasped.

My father's anger pacified, but a sad, meek, resentful colour covered his face. He pressed mother's hand and twirled his fingers through her hair and uncannily blinking his eyes looked towards the tattered roof of the house. I sat next to him looking at his strong body. But nothing was in the catch of my understanding. Suddenly, he stood up and asked me, 'Where is Maya?' I had no answer as I didn't know where Maya had been all this time. He went out of the home and cried, 'Maya, where are you? Maya—Maya?' Maya didn't respond her presence nearby place. He came in and scolded me, 'Can't you look after her? She is always left at home at your risk?' But I had no answer? He again had a brief round outside and came back.

Maya entered home smilingly and lovingly looking at father, she jumped into his lap, and, embracing her to his chest, he kissed and kissed and kissed. Maya laughed and said, 'Baba, how hot outside?' He again kissed her, 'Where have you been all this time?' Maya described her play with her friend in bubbling words and tried to play with father's broad moustache and said, 'Maa, I want meal?' Mother was not in a condition to even speak but said, Wait, just I give you,' and turned around. She tried to sit but severe pain in her waist turned down her effort. 'Take rest. I'll do myself a little for meal. Will you take tea first?' the father said and rose from his place and prepared tea and gave it to my mother. My father prepared a meal that day and I helped him. All of us devoured upon the meal.

My uncle remained fiercely hostile thereafter.
And my father swallowed his pride
to keep mother's word.
I learnt a lesson: *kshama virasya bhushanam!*

FATHER, THOU ART A MAN,
WHO KNOWS HOW TO AIM AN ARROW.
FATHER, THOU ART A MAN,
WHO KNOWS HOW TO PLOUGH
A LONELY FURROW.

My uncle's cruel and brutal deed imprinted
a deep wound into my heart.
It deeply disturbed me.
Why brother is always a foe to brother?
Sons of one womb; never learn a bit from honeycomb.
It was not certainly an event one
could sweep under the carpet.

I saw a couple with one child sitting
on the nearby bench.
She was a woman of nearly thirty; somewhat obese, dark-skinned, but fashionable. She looked sulky, stubborn, bored; engrossed in thought, she blurted her thick lips as if she was abusing somebody impertinently. A child of around 3 years was playing with her *sari's pallu*. The child's lean and weak body was covered with heavy but costly garments. And that young man, her husband, was looking outside at drizzle unenthusiastically. He was slim, meek, and silent, and partly bald, dressed in ordinary clothes, a checked blue shirt and a cream-colour trousers. A kind of a grief had blackened his dark face. But she looked bold and arrogant. Why so strange lines were sparkling on her face? Why was he so restless and baffled?

They began their talk.

'Everything has a limit, you know?' she began.

'Hum!' he sighed deeply.

'The limit is over! I won't listen to your word hereafter? Will you do all these in your old age if not now? No time to spare now. My child will go to school after just three years. We've to start his education. And do you have any idea that simply for the admission of any convent school, thousands of rupees have to be spent! And I've to send my child to *sibbesi* (CBSE) pattern school; you better understand? Twenty-five thousand *saaheb*— hear! Minimum twenty-five thousand rupees are to be paid for the admission to the good convent school, and remaining fees for the whole year is extra—*sshit!*'

He looked, just for a while, at her tremulously, but he dared not speak. Instead, he started playing his fingers with a collar of his shirt, looking out at the echoing grunts and groans of the buses that were rushing into the parking lanes of the bus station. Strange it should be so ambient to see someone writhing in strange agony! And after all, the weather was so revengeful outside.

'Whatever is it?' she continued in a rustled tone, 'Twenty-five or thirty, no matter? I must send my child to only *sibbesi pattern*. You spend a big amount of money on your father and mother, and have no money for your own son? Not enough, is it? How much do you squander on your brother and sisters: their college fees, their tuition fees, their clothes, their books, their travel, and what not? You pay for their trifle expenditures and have no money for my only son? Tell you, listen my words—take a loan either or do whatever? Warn you to keep ready the sum of thirty-five thousand rupees before this summer?'

Then he was stashed with a shame and
hesitated even to look around.

Daring troubled him.

He bent down his neck and kept his eyes down to the dirty-tiled floor, seemed far away from the world.

A poor husband!

'My son,' she started with her harsh words, 'is three now. Three more years to wait for him. Are you listening to my words, the words I'm barking for all this time? Finish at least two more works till then—purchase one plot and build our own house. Prices of real estate and material are mounting up day by day.'

She stared at him with angry red eyes.

He was quiet, silent.

He might be meditating in reclusive repentance;
marriage was nothing but repentance for him.

Something very extraordinary made him
so frightened, surely! I guessed.

'Can we live without house? Our own house is must! Own house is the place of happy life, you know! You do whatever you can? Take loan, sell farm, or do whatever, but you build house first. Fed up! I'm fed up by living in that old house—completely fed up!' looking around, she said hysterically.

Her eyes reflected severe anger and restlessness.

He was caught in a straw that broke
the camel-back-like situation.
With bewildered expression on the face, he lifted
his eyes up and hesitatingly murmured, 'I'll talk
at home.' There was a slight scorn that sounded
in his voice. He was really caught in the mire.

'At home or here, does remain the same thing! Do we get any privacy or mental peace, silence, or feel easy at home even? Everybody keeps a watch on my doings and spies on our talk,' raising her voice, she continued, 'All hunt down our discussion like perspicacious hunters. All take pleasure in eavesdropping our talk! And do I get even a minute for my own work? Remain busy in housework all twenty-four hours. My god, no rest! Luckily, I got time here to say something; no matter on this bus stand. You're really an inactive and insolent man; a drone indeed! Wasting your time in nothing-doing! Now, your salary is up. Sixth pay commission is implemented already and seventh will be declared soon. Can't you deduct some money from your salary on the house loan premiums until ten years up to *Balya's* tenth? Listen, man's will should be strong and man should not be a dull dog! It's a bit much tolerance for me! A penny spent is a penny earned; that all I know! Just now, I have completed my B. Ed. and still am killing flies at home! No, I won't sit at home hereafter! I'll be out to join a job, whatever! My head is too tired to waste time sitting at home!'

She, then, straightened her attire and
glued then to the same topic.

She had to dig her nails into her hands, so as
not to console on the present situation much.
How difficult it was for him to control her!
He appeared to be a taciturn, tongue-
tied, serious young man!

'I sorted out an information that teachers' posts are being advertised nowadays, but in non-aided schools,' she flowed down with a bunch of sharp words in reverse, 'No use to spend money on getting a job in such non-aided schools, you know? Instead, it's better to join as a *shikshan sevak*—isn't it? The rates are mounting up day by day. Even ten to twelve lacs are not sufficient today! For getting a teacher's job, we've to spend at least twenty to twenty-five lacks? All right, you can skip away from this today. But tomorrow? Some of my friends have joined as *shikshan sevak* already and enjoying their life fully. That's called the real life, you know? And look at me; nothing, me a lazy bee. I'm cooking *bhakri* and *subji*, burning hands on griddle; doing works from cleaning leftover dirty dishes to cleaning floors; doing all for mother-in-law and father-in-law ; working for those tiny creatures like brother and sister; wasting time unnecessarily at home? I'd many wishes and aspirations of my own before marriage; but no, all this came to my fate, and fate is all powerful. My father always kept on advising me to take care of own career and emphasised always a point of earning money as money is a backbone of man's life, but everything is all neglected here; all waste of time and no hard work.

Waste of time and waste of energy. Outside the world is pacing up rapidly. Ample is to do. Ample ways can bring us money. And prosperity lies in money. Wake up! Wake up, my dear! Time is a friend, but time can also be a foe, if not rightly paced up.'

Hardly, he could resist himself and, accumulating
a bouncy courage, spoke a few words.
Pugnacious spouse versus peaceable spouse.
A combat of words.
Word led to word and there occurred
a quarrel-like situation.

She was speaking very comatosely. She was too shameless to have any awareness about the public around. Was it wise to wash dirty linen in public? Her small kid pissed against her *sari* and jumped quickly on the floor and began to cry with widely opening mouth. But she didn't care. She lifted her kid up and started to calm him. But no use! And her style of calming the child made me to laugh even in that rancorous condition.

Her impertinent deportment made me woeful and impervious.

He tried to control himself.

Almost imperceptibly, he covered his face with his palms. He needed fresh impetus to start thereafter. Womanhood showed him its power. He might have been thinking how to do away with that extravagant situation. Weren't they leading a cat's and dog's life? And if luck were persistent, he was down in his luck!

Like a wounded soldier, he wanted
to throw down the gauntlet.

'Living at home like a rotten rag recede me every time,' she reprimanded severely. 'Sheer waste of time! A kind of revenge against self. There is no dearth of jobs. Search is must. And I want job anyhow. Won't sit at home lazily? I'll definitely start tuitions—I'm sure. Whatever, Science or Math or English or Marathi? I want money. I want job. I want free life. Am I a caged bird?'

No change occurred in her. She had
been irresistible indeed!

He was playing a role of the kind listener.

'Too late, we're in fact—too late! All are going speedily ahead of us,' words became slaves of her tongue, 'plots, plots, and plots; your friends, your relatives, all are purchasing plot after plot. All are building houses. Many are buying lands, and you? You're just clearing tears by your knuckles. Am I wrong? House, you build house first. I tell you. I've my own desires. I desire to live a free life. So, make me free—I tell you! I want to leave that house. I don't like that dirty old man called father-in-law. I can't work for him playing as an obedient servant. And tell those worst people called brother and sister to respect me. This is my last warning ; you must remember!'

Her stringent words made him intolerant.

'I'll do everything for you and set right the situation,' greatly distressed, he summed up his courage, 'but this is not a place where you're talking all about. Absurdity!

It does appear insane! Wait to get it right! Don't be
impatient!'

'Don't be impatient! O, man, what are you talking
about! What are you doing for? All these four years,
what am I doing then?' she rebuked harshly, 'Say, don't
be impatient! I won't listen your *faltu* barking. Crossed
the limit already! Warn you, sell out all lands of your
name and adjust money for my job, you know? Watch
the time! Time seldom presents any chance!'

And looking at her costly *sari*, she crossed her
fingers and tried to set her beautiful locks stylishly.

'No, I won't sell out,' he said firmly.

'Why? What be done with that land and all?'

'No, it's not a proper time for it.'

'What do you say? Proper time! Know, know, I know
your all plans. Am I gone mad? And I'm sure, if you
do something for me, I'll eat my hat,' she ridiculed his
words and laughed clumsily.

'Yes, I say, it's not a proper time for it,' he tried to
tighten his grip.

'Tell me then, when that proper time will come?' she
mimicked his words.

'Yes, when that will come, I'll take decision.'

'Oh, you know the art of decision making then—really?'

'I agree to do whatever for you, but jib at making such
a speech here,' in a silent tone, he said.

But that fussy woman flowed down
with sharper words in reverse.

'Do whatever, but I won't wait? That's final,' she warned
him.

Dark pangs lodged on his face.

'How many days have been elapsed for the mother's death?' sadly, said he.

'Mother's death? It's suicide. Who asked her to die? Gone,willingly committing suicide. She died of not any disease, but of her own act? Why then this much sorrowful cries? So much mourning? Death is certain. And if somebody decides to go of her own, who can avoid the happening? And, tell me, how was her life so profitable for anybody in the house? Always coughing, coughing. and coughing and rolling on like a walking medicine shop? All house was greatly disturbed. So, why should we waste time, sitting all the time uselessly by putting hands on forehead and tearing down on a useless death?' she criticised.

Startled words of that woman hurt me deeply
and overdosed my concept of marriage.

I thought that that man was not over-aged. He might be of my age. His sad face and sad life made me think more on life, especially on married life. Her hatred for her mother-in-law annoyed me acutely.

His mother committed suicide.
The word suicide rang the bell of alarm in my ears.
Miserable is man and woman!

By sunset, like a great lonely person, I stalked towards Hemant's big bungalow. Beyond all doubt, it was confirmed to have a great welcome (insulting indeed) by someone at home; Ketki surely, his wife.

It must be admitted that that was my daring effort to reach his home for an urgent enquiry of his ailing mother. I had lost all my reputation as a friend of him and thus it was my first visit to his home after three months. Ketki had warned me not to step in her home for any work. My condition was exactly like a muddle-brained metaphysician, who by some strange freak of courage stepped in by deviating the warning of (the home minister). The more I strengthened my decision to meet his mother, the more I trembled to enter the home. But anyhow, I had to meet my mother (yes, I treated Hemant's mother as my mother).

Hemant had married Ketki four years ago. But their marriage proved an unhappy union. In the first few days, it went smoothly, but soon the quarrel-treats dashed in. Hemant, the only son of a rich farmer of my village, acquired everything by dint of his hard work and wisdom. He was a poet of great repute and just had received the Maharashtra State Award for his poetry collection 'Ant Nahi Kalokhala?' Most good and greater part of Hemant's ten years of fame as poet, he had brought a name and fame to the village. Committed to the severe pains and pangs of the farmers, he wrote many award-winning poems and stamped his mark on Modern Marathi Poetry. I always called him a revolutionary idealist.

He was tall and handsome, sane and simple, considerate and committed, young boy of my age, and my classmate up to higher secondary education. He did his MA (Marathi) from Nagpur University standing first merit and had cleared NET and SET examinations, but had no inclination to work as lecturer, instead he desired to be a poet. He had not been a prolific writer but astutely penned down competitive significant poetry. After all, he was a good orator. His father, a highly disciplined and dedicated farmer, died of cancer suddenly after a month of his marriage. And his mother, a beautiful woman in the village, was left to suffer the loss of her life partner. 'How generous and magnanimous woman his mother is!' I always exclaimed for her generosity. I loved her at the same intensity as I loved my own mother. Considering me as one of the members of their family, Hemant's father and mother trusted me keenly and even entrusted me a work to find a good girl of their caste, who would suit to Hemant's personality as a wife. I always accompanied Hemant for seeing the girls, but his maternal uncle played a game and finalised his marriage with his only daughter, Ketki.

Ketki, short and smutty girl, was two years older than him and had never been a match to him in any respect. Right from her beginning as a wife, she left no mark of a good woman, instead, she proved herself as a snobbish, proud, vainglorious, and ill-hearted woman. Intensively loquacious, she used to throttle anybody's mouth and always had an edge over. I simply could not think that a boy who wrote so charmingly and informingly about the sufferings of farmers would live a very troubled life.

He was out of home those days for to attending Akhil Bharatiya Sahitya Sammelan at Pune. Patiently, with the tact and plan and understanding of the most experienced, most exquisitely sympathetic visitor, I entered his home (a big old wada). Wasudeo, a middle-aged worker, came forward and bade me,' Namaste'. A black and fat dog, Moti welcomed me by lifting up his front legs on my chest and licking his long tongue in acquainted affection. Wasudeo asked me to sit on the chair. I sat quietly. It wasn't worth the effort; nothing was worth the effort. I began to count the minutes in reverse. My paralysing act denounced me to stay there, but I stayed. For a while, I was thoroughly penetrated with the sense of guilt. I was always afraid (secretly, of course, and without admitting it) of Ketki that she might scold me and laugh at me (being an unmarried fellow, surely).

'Wot is wot, Wasudeo?' Ketki's voice roared. 'Woo's there at this time?'

Wasudeo quickly ran into the drawing hall.

Time passed by. I waited.

Strange! I dreamed I was in a wood—somewhere far away from, really, human habitation!

And I was awaiting a tigress!

What a terrible dream! I had always had such terrible dreams whenever I had been there.

Strange!

After some time, softly without a sound, a dirty and dark curtain rolled up, and Ketki came out.

I stood up from my chair and greeted her, but she overlooked and took the pin out of her hair and smiled. 'Wot are yer putting it in here for?' she questioned in her snobbish and rustic style.

At her question I stared out of the veranda, shinning with twilight, faintly twitching my nose.
'To meet my mother,' I replied sadly.
'Oh, to yer mother!' she mimicked my words.
'Much time has passed for my last visit to her,' I said.
'I ever doubt yer word?' she said obliquely.
'How is she?' I dared speak a little.
She stood, pleating the frills of her expensive gown, and glancing from one to the other things scattered around, like a wounded tiger. She then blubbered for an unknown name and clasped her hands as if she were rejoicing for some special event. It sounded a ridiculous situation, but it was useless to attempt to interfere.

One slim black cat suddenly jumped down the roof and mewed pitifully as if it were caught in trouble.
'Don't care! Don't care! Yer mother is all right, I tells!' she spoke rapidly.
'Shall I meet her?' I asked.
'Wot for?' said she, scratching her head.
'Well, for the past few days I haven't seen her.'
'Oh, past few days an' months of them! I tells yer, ye've broken my words, my warning!'

She clutched her head with her hands and stared with blazing eyes at me like a mad woman. Every moment, hatred grew more vivid in her eyes and her words sounded obfuscating. The light grew darker and it was almost dark. Wasudeo switched on the light and the veranda flashed in. But for her, the dark did not matter. She was harder than the rock that time, but for me it was a tough hardness. Suddenly, Moti started barking and running to and fro. 'What's that? What's up? Wasudeo ran after Moti and clutched tightly and belted him.

'Yes, remember your warning, but understand me—I want to meet my mother.' I requested her.

'I think I must be mad. I tells yer, ye must have had a presentiment, I think. Oh, a strong believer of presentiment ye're! But, tells yer, 'thing will happen! Won't permit you to meet that woman in absence of yer friend? Better to walk yer way back?' she said firmly and asked Wasudeo to bring a glass of water for me.

Wasudeo hastily walked the way to the kitchen.

'No, thank you,' I said and rose from the chair.

'Don't yer think, it's bad to meet a woman in absence of 'er husband?' her voice was full of unknown doubt.

'Sorry!' said I meekly.

She shook her head.

I thought I saw what was so ugly, so extraordinary that no really sane man could dignify it.

Suddenly, I became aware of my nakedness and unworthiness and quickly moved back to the gate.

'Don't misunderstand me. Have yer glass of water or would complain against me for yer not getting a glass of water even—in friend's house?' she smiled, but rudely.

I walked back home.

It was after a week only, on my journey to Nagpur,
the news of his mother's death pierced my ears.

WHO HAS SEEN A GOD?
AND WHERE IS GOD'S HOME?
SEE GOD IN MOTHER'S FACE,
WHO KILLS HATE WITH A MACE.

Fifteen minutes passed by.
That woman made me to think of the
sudden death of Hemant's mother.

Calculatingly, she was Ketki's perfect match. Like a
hunted beast, Ketki behaved with me that day. With
every minute that passed, the face and figure of
Ketki was rushing into my eyeballs like a delayed
train entering the crowded and bustling terminus. It
was distinctly evil luck for Hemant, who really was
thoroughly respectable at heart, that he and his wife
should run into the callous unhappy married life.
Complications and complications made his life worse.
His life fell into the hands of such a spiral woman that
even with any special desire he would not overtake a
speck of it. The brutal directness of Ketki's behaviour
aroused a certain combative derision in the Hemant's
dreamy life. And his mother, most respectable woman
in the village, passed her last days like a slave. Her
desires for her only son's married life actively turned to
be a maxim: *If wishes were horses, beggars would ride.*
Never in her life she bore anybody, no grudge, no scorn,

no malice! She had a hard life after her son's marriage. Terrible it had been!

The wall clock was ticking the seconds
and minutes and hours.
Overlooking the vivid people and observing vivacity
of daily life, I was still standing at the pillar.
Revulsion engrossed my thinking power having
listened to that woman's disgusting words.
Had she any respect for people?
That other side of a woman thrashed me back to home.
Mother's face appeared in my eyes.
Her condition quaked me with fear; her tears
threatened me; her body ruffled me.

—mother—mother—her illness—growing day by day—her treatment—costly—spent money—but insufficient—doctors—didn't say—thing clearly—but—some of her gland—has become inflamed—abscess is forming—she suffered—severe attacks—attacks—deadly—diagnosis—of doctor—remains—doubt—doubt—medicines *n* medicines—she gulps—*x ray*—*ct scan*—*mri*—all failed—to detect—her disease— all went in vain—useless—progress of—medical science—poor man's malady—hard-working woman—became bedridden—doubts—but her falling health—mounting up—many advised—wrong methods—for cure—villagers—have such evil notions—for cure—but—what risky way—mother never cared—for her health—works—works—works—never open her heart—no complaint—always stressing—point of education—she wants—her children educated—she dreams—to see—her daughters—happy—married—she has—see her only son—employed—on higher post—ready—do any work—for her children's welfare—education—helps—*maya*—*mamta*—adjusts money—last month—she gave me—two thousand rupees—on my demand—for examination fees—asked me—not to inquire—*n*—her only son—33-year old son—qualified son—partly—employed son—can't help her— relies still—on her hard earned money—not yet able—to earn—bread *n* butter—shameful act—surely shameful—that divorcee daughter—*maya*—how does—she bear—daughter's pains—mother—always—my mother—wished—to marry—*maya*—gracefully—she resisted—herself—to any expenditure—but—her dream—her wish—to marry her daughter—with good boy—shattered—soon—after few—months—of her marriage—her daughter's—life devastated—*maya*—came back home—*n*—mother's health—begins—to worsen—diminishing—day by day—

My deep thoughts were broken at the sight of
a woman, who dashed me from the back.
Controlling myself, I looked at her
and helped her to stand.
She needed help. She seemed quite exhausted.

She sat on the floor gasping. She was writhing in pain.
Something echoed inside me: *Give her a helping hand,*

she is your mother! My vitality was much too low that moment for my bad health, but I thought I must help her. Bending down, I asked her, 'Do you want water?' I ran towards ST Bus canteen, which was overcrowded, but anyhow I managed to get a glass of water and came back to her. She drank water voluptuously, sighed and looked at me approvingly. Her chest was bellowing like blacksmith's bellows.

There rose a slight brightness in her eyes. 'I think you're a perfect angel for giving me water right time,' she stammered. Dimly, she looked at me. 'That's my duty, mother,' said I beseechingly. 'Growing age is always serious,' said she and tried to control her aching body.

She looked quite cultured.

'How do you feel now?'

'Little fair!'

'Wait, I bring tea for you?' said I without caring for a little amount of money in my pocket.

'No, don't care for that! Well, I'm well now! I have to catch a bus for my village. Must reach home before evening,' she said.

Severe attack of coughing troubled her much.

'You're not well. Try to reach home early, mother,' I said.

'You're quite a good boy, saying me mother!' she looked at me.

'Where have you to go?'

'Nandura. Missed my passenger train, thus, came to catch a bus.'

'Okay. I look for your bus. Stay here.'

'No. I know the bus timing. My bus will come at two o'clock.'

'Oh, take rest then,' I said.

She muttered to herself and threw sidelong glances at the bumping crowd, her cheeks were puffed up under the crisscross of wrinkles, her lips were sulking, and her broad eyes blinked smoothly. She was trying to calm down her breathing, and suppressing the murmur of exhaustion with care, she spoke to me with complete composure, and the tenderness in her weak eyes was quite captive. She had a tender word and gentle look. She straightened her legs, clearing specks of dirt on the floor with her hands, and rested a while.

'Why is it unnecessarily raining today?' she complained.

'That's we call a bad luck for farmers!' I seconded her words.

'Today is Ghatsthapana Day—a day of Maa Durga's arrival!'

'Right, but what a man can do?'

'Maa Durga might shower her blessings on drought-affected farmers. That is god's will!' she prayed.

'Mother, our prayers go up, but His blessings never shower upon us,' I said.

'No, His blessings ever shower upon us. One should have an eye to look at, my son!' she explained.

'My mother also has so deep a faith in god!'

'Mothers are born to pray god only. There is a deep, thick line on every mother's palm; she is born to suffer,' she coughed again.

'I don't know where god is? I see god in my mother's face,' I said apparently.

'So much do you love your mother?' she asked.

She examined my face closely with her adoring look.

'My mother is pretty and kind, noble and simple.'

'Believe, my son, every mother is pretty and kind, noble and simple as you said,' she spoke sadly.

'Yes, mother! I believe!'

'You're a good son! B-ut, b-ut . . .' she stuttered a while.

'But?' I asked anxiously.

'But, every son is not same as you - not same – as – y-ou.'

Tears welled up to her eyes.

'Do you have a son, mother?' I asked.

'Three sons,' she tried to clear rolling tears from her tainted cheeks.

'Why then these tears in your eyes, mother?' I became more inquisitive.

'All three are three different directions. Never can't meet and nobody can unite them.'

'Why are they so parted?'

'My man (*husband*) committed suicide last year because of their regular quarrel for land, and we've only ten acres of land. Two are married and the younger is quite a rubbish fellow caught in a bad company. Heavily he drinks and passes time and sometimes beats me. Married sons never care for me. They live their own lives with their wives and children. And I am landless now—live barely—a widow—lonely—cursed life—I say—cursed life,' she said and tried her hand into her small bag.

Quickly, she rose up, and looking lovingly at me, she put her hand on my head and said, 'Take care of your mother. Man can buy everything in the world's market, but can't buy mother from any market—see! Be happy; be successful.'

She stood up, blessed me, and went out of
the bus station without caring for rain.
Acute bafflement seized me.
After that old woman's departure from there,
there stood my mother again in my eyes.

The last day of twelfth standard examination.
I was glad to tell my mother and father the news of my good performance in the entire examination. I could perform very well in all the papers. The moment I left the examination centre, I conceived an idea of presenting some sweets to my parents as a token of their love and great pains and pangs they had been going through. I was eager to reach home, and thus in a great haste, I reached the famous Blue Star Sweet Mart *of the town; read the board of items, and thrashed my hand into the trousers' pocket; took out a twenty-rupee note; calculated the sum to be paid for the sweets; and asked the man on the counter to give quarter kilogram peda. I thought myself a very smart boy who could serve his parents by offering peda as a token of love and great pains put in by his father and mother for educating him. I thought myself a great worshipper who was going to offer a great worship to his gods—father and mother.*

A priceless offering indeed!

But, I saw one chit of paper stuck with a twenty-rupee note, and that was doctor's prescription of medicine for mother. I read a long list of medicines, hesitated a while, and asked the counter man to cancel the order given for the peda, instead I made up my mind to purchase some medicine for mother. But, how to purchase a long list of medicine only in twenty rupees and the medicine's prices were unaffordable for a poor man. How priceless was a twenty rupee note for me! Restricting my earnest wish of offer, I controlled my taste, and I walked towards a medicine shop. The market was beautifying its business with all kinds of people.

I, confining mother's face in my eyes, strolled the way by calculating the prices of medicine.

Suddenly, I came across Kashinath Patil, a village farmer, who stood in front of a big cloth store. I went to him and said, 'Namaste, uncle.'

He looked at me and said, 'Arrey, baap re! Just thinking someone to help me and you came before me! Actually, god sent you for my help.'

His face sparkled with quite a relaxed expression and apt elation.

I never saw such an elation and relaxed expression on my father's face in all these years.

He said, 'Babu (my pet name), it's very good that you meet me. Here, come. We'll go inside the cloth store.'

'Uncle, what you've to purchase?' I asked.

I knew Kashinath Patil well.

'Arrey, Lugada!' Kashinath Patil said and smiled gracefully, twirling his bushy moustache stylishly.

His gleeful face made me think of my father.

When shall I see such a gleeful and graceful face of my father?

We entered into the cloth store. One middle-aged man came to us and asked us to sit in a corner place. I was awestruck to see that big showroom lighted with many bulbs and full bottom racks of beautiful variety of clothes. The salesman asked, 'Okay, what do you want, Patil—suiting, shirting, sari?'

Kashnath Patil looked at me and hinted me to speak my wise words.

'Lugada!' I said.

'Okay, up to what price?' asked the salesman.

'Show us first,' Kashinath Patil said.

'Okay, we've a good and ample variety of lugadas, but I want to know your affordable range of price. How much can you pay for?' looking askance on us, the salesman said.

'You first show us, we'll tell you then?' said Kashinath Patil firmly. I agreed on his words.

Kashnath Patil was quite infamous for his reckless nature, a very devious and deranged man.

'Okay!' said the salesman and spread a line of lugadas of vivid colours before us.

It was not the first time I came for purchasing lugada. I came with my father for two or three times and my father always said that I had a good choice of colours and had a fine eye for texture-testing of clothes.

A matured little man!

'See, this range then? It goes on seven hundred rupees and above,' said the salesman with eyes full in sparkling pride.

'You don't worry for the range and money; you show only,' said Kashinath Patil confidently.

He smiled in his cheeks.

His face glaringly manifested vainglorious lines.

'Look, this is nine hundred and above,' said the salesman and looked with doubtful eyes at us. I hadn't seen such a costly range of clothes ever before, but wished for it for my mother.

'No, show of lesser price,' Kashinath Patil changed his mood.

'How much—that's I'm asking you,' the salesman asked spreading his businesslike smile.

'Nearing five hundred,' Kashinath Patil said.

'See, this is five hundred range,' said the salesman and showed a pair of red and green colour. Very attractive colours!

My eyes fixed on the red lugada—my mother's favourite colour.

My mother also needed a new lugada urgently. But Kashinath Patil looked reluctant to agree with the prices. He instantly changed his mood and hinted me to go out quickly of the cloth store. And then hastily we went out for no reason. (He is not a simple man, but avaricious and crafty, does everything for his own, and never comes to any decision after having bargain or purchase, a kind of a cunning purchaser.) He then took me to three more cloth stores, wasted time in testing the prices, reversed his mood, and finally did nothing, instead, he said, 'No, this market isn't good, no good quality of worth purchasing. Babu, my mood is damn bad; you can go back wherever you want to?'

Then saying, 'I'm late. I'll have to get a move on,' he walked back on his way.

I didn't understand what was happening.

In a sudden stroke of idea, I ran after to catch him. Caring not for a collision by a running motorcycle, and heavy abuse by the motorcyclist, I caught him at the door of one small restaurant, which was full of people enjoying samosas, idlis, wadas, bhujia, sevia, tea.

'Uncle, uncle!' I stammered.

'Yes?' he asked.

'Uncle?' I couldn't sum up words.

'Tell, early, I've many works to do?' he said and looked at me.

He sensed a doubt and became cautious.

But, how to ask him for my demand?

I was quite in a dilemma. Stood numb for a while!

The market was in full swing.

I went near him and opened my mouth to demand fifty rupees for mother's medicine—but, suddenly, my father's words resonated into my ears, 'Never borrow money from others until you're in a jinx,' and I awoke. Kashinath Patil was in haste. I moved back on my way. Kashinath Patil didn't ask me any word. He might have got the clue?

   I dared not purchase medicine for short of money, squashed the revolt of thoughts going on in my head and made my way back to the bus station, then hurried to reach home. Even twenty rupees note was quite valuable for me. I held that note before my eyes and swore to study more to achieve the next goal in education. I thought it was a great hardship for me. My father's words awoke me: 'Don't grieve over hardships, because hardships make a man.'

Filled with a kind of vigour and energy, dreaming a great dream of life, I walked on the road.

   'I know conscience is a good friend and one who listens to it more often becomes a good man. My father, like a good teacher, always warns me not to weep inside the mind because it's dangerous; rather, it's better to weep open. I want to make my home, with my persistence, the centre and not the boundary of affection. I know the road of life is very long and what looks like the end is more often just a bend in the road, so walk on the road of life tirelessly until the last destination is arrived. I want to grab more and more opportunities in life on the line of my father's advice and teaching. My great teacher is my father. Carry on boy, carry on!' I befitted to my views.

After thirty minutes of travel, I got off the bus and walked on the way home.

The sinking sun accelerated my steps to reach home early. Suddenly, a flock of crows appeared and began to circle—caw, caw, caw! And my steps were filled with an awful fear. 'Why the crows cawing?' A strange shiver trembled my whole body. 'I haven't seen such a flock of crows earlier, because crows are rarely seen even in the field nowadays. Even the sparrows and many birds aren't seen because of excessive use of poisonous insecticides in the fields,' thoughts barricaded my mind. That time of evening and the harsh cawing of crows devastated my courage and hurriedly I began almost running home.

A new danger was before my eyes.
I stepped into the home and my
eyes fixed on my mother.

She was weeping, laying herself on the dead body of a buffalo. Mamta hugged me in fear. Maya was silently seated at mother's feet. Tears and tears! I put my hand on mother's shoulder and asked, 'When did it happen, Maa?' Mother couldn't control her tears and began to cry more loudly. After a careful look at the foaming mouth of the buffalo, I came to know the reason. Yet I exclaimed, 'Maa, how terrific it is!' Mother sobbed and, controlling herself, said, 'Babu, Babu, my Mohna died—she went leaving us in trouble—snake bitten her—died.'

Dreamed that night I was walking to
the market—buffalo market.

—a long—parade of—buffalo—buffalos—black—grey—green—red—violet—blue—white—and—silver—and golden—vivid colours—and—four horns—four ears—eight legs—and—wings—broad

mouth—and—thick fur—on neck—small eyes—all
eating—bhakri—flesh—mud—crying—crying—
crying—for bhakri—for human flesh—like human-
being—dancing—jumping—   joking—jerking—
drinking—blood—blood—human blood—laughing—
like—thunder— smelling—smelling—human flesh—
bleeding mouth—crying—like—child for blood—
queer bit—costly garments—they—wear—dance—
run—play—making—circle—around—father—
laughing—laughing—singing—son--beggar—
beggar—thou—art—beggar—kiss—see—my dear—
beautiful clothes—we wear—see—see—see—see
my master—wake—*n*—hear—great blaster—*n*—big
buffalo—growing big—bigger—biggest—growing—
again—growing—*n*—falling down—on ground—
buffalos—buffalos—catching—all   catching—
mother—embracing—hugging—kissing—bloody
mouth— dancing—dancing—running—around—
around—around

Strange, very strange dream!
Mohna, my mother's pet buffalo, was a
real source of home expenditure.
Mohna was not an animal for us but
one of the members of our family.
The great loss?

MOTHER, THOU ART A CHILD
OF EARTH AND SKY.
LIMITLESS IS THY LOVE AND CARE!

MOTHER, THOU ART A LADY
WITH NATURE SHY.
KIND IS THY HEART AND FACE FAIR!

I saw one old man sitting at the
corner of the opposite bench.

Hoping to get a place, I walked there and requested the old man to adjust a little place. He was quite a good old man. I sat beside him. I looked at his wrinkled face. He was dimly looking at rain outside.

Looking restlessly around the bus station, that old man covered his hands into the front long pockets of his ash colour sweater. He was quite a handsome old man. Richly whitish complexion and brilliant white beard and long ears made his face so attractive! He averted his eyes and tried to think of something that wasn't fair to calculate the crowd. He looked quite a resourceful person and cultured and rightly modest. The expression on his face was one of contemptuous amusement. He turned his bleak eyes coolly this way and that over the crowd and murmured some words into his cheeks. Becoming aware of my inquisitive glances, he turned to me and asked me in his deep and husky voice, 'You look much worried?'

'No! Nothing's like that!' I replied quickly.

'Eyes can't hide anything.'

'Because of travel—'

'Did you cry?' he asked.

'No!' I lied.

'Eyes can't hide anything!' he repeated.

'Because of sleep—'

'Did you mourn?' he interrupted my words.

'No!' I lied again.

'Eyes can't hide anything!' he repeated the same version.

Grim bafflement invaded my face.

'Are you an employed man?'

'No,' said I quickly.

And he reflected his strong embarrassment.

'Not yet?'

'Not yet?' I replied.

'What age are you running?'

'Thirty-three!'

'Single or married?'

'Single?'

'Don't you feel you're being late?'

'For what?'

'Be in sense, boy! I'm asking you about your marriage?'

'Of course, I'm late.'

'What's your father?'

'Farmer.'

'How many acres of land?'

'Seven acres.'

'Mother?'

'She is quite a hard-working mother.'

Tongue blocked my words.

'Siblings?'

'Two sisters; younger.'

'What they do?'

I looked askance on him.

'You're not looking very well, dear fellow?' he added after a moment's pause sighing.

'A little tired, that's all?'

'Worried?' he sympathetically asked.

'No?'

'No, there's certainly a cause?'

'Tension of interview may be stupefying?' said I.

'Right, because your face took on expression of anxiety, even of alarm!' he read my face rightly.

'Can one be glad and sorry at the same time?'

'Nice question? But, I think positively, I see the style of this thing and I'm sure one can be!'

His eyes sparkled with a sudden alacrity.

Something broke inside him. He found himself commensurate with age and experience and sobbing with silent, painful, and somewhat civilised smile. He took out a handkerchief of his trousers' pocket and pressed to his mouth. I thought he was just his bright natural self. I knew he liked to talk to me. I never knew why the Indians dipped into the deep inquiry of family matters. There followed a long silence and then there was the beginning of a serious conversation on life, portending the pre-positivistic epoch of kindliness and absurdity of human life.

'You said of tension of interview, just now?' he continued.

'Right?'

'Life is also a difficult interview!'

'Right?'

'I always try myself to distinguish between *Character is destiny* and *Destiny is character*, but so far couldn't reach to any justification,' he eluded and held his right palm before his eyes. 'Seventy-ninth winter is running over my body, and still am testing and calculating these dictums. Man's birth is certainly, the die is cast. Life is a serious business.'

Leaning back in his bench, he laughed, but I found his laugh frank and free, wholly agile.

Then, silently driving his right hand into the trousers' pocket, he took out a small case.

He stared after him for a while and sighed.

'See, this is my *destiny*?' he said, taking one tablet out of the small case.

'It's medicine.'

'It's my life.'

'Why do you say it's your *destiny*?'

'Because it's my life partner who controls my life.'

'Will you, please, explain the difference between *destiny* and *fate*?' I asked.

'Nice, but a tougher question! What I should explain about *fate* is: the bad things that will happen to somebody. And *destiny* slightly differs in meaning: the things that will happen to somebody in the future, especially things that one cannot change or avoid. More or less both the terms are nearest in meaning,' he explained.

'In this case, *destiny* is a vital term!' I asked.

'Of course, *destiny* is vital!' he agreed.

I observed he made a successful effort to control his words.

'So long a life you led and abundant experience brought in compatibility in you.'

'You think so?'

'You're a mindful man.'

'And reclusive, too.'

'Why?'

'People say so!'

'If it is so, it must bear a reason?' I opined frankly.

'When does a man lead a lonely life?' he asked.

'When?' I jibbed.

'When a man is running many problems in his life!'

'Right, sir!'

'In me, there lies rusticity!'

'But, you look a civilised man!'

'Civilised man can be a good counsellor, but a bad commander!' he smiled in the fashion of an expert spy.

'You speak quite resourcefully,' I admired his words.

'Resources are nothing but the sorted bunches of experience that man accumulates during his lifetime. Man always should speak frank and free words because when people are suspicious with you, you start being suspicious with them. Thus, every man should spy a destructive figure in the distance.'

He seemed a squeaky clean person.

He became silent then.

'It's fine to hear your informative words!' I said sincerely.

'Which post are you going to appear for an interview?' he changed the course of talk.

'For assistant professor in English,' I replied promptly.

'Dirty business?' he remarked stringently.

'I'm trying for this post for the last six years.'

'God bless you for gyrating so much tolerance, my boy!' he pressed his palms softly.

'Tolerance is the weapon for the poor!'

'That's why I said *dirty business*?'

'So, what one can do?'

'Isn't it a fake to run after the teacher's post at present?'

'So what a qualified young aspirator can do?'

'Employment has become a burning issue nowadays. What I know about this is that teachers' absenteeism in the schools and colleges and private tutoring are the main adversaries to present education system. The practice of ghost teachers, the overall changed attitude of education management, involvement of teachers in mismanagement, and many more attitudes can be considered as other grey areas in education system,' he summed up his highly informative and scholastic words.

'Right, sir! Is there no pity sitting in the clouds?'

'I can't help saying tries to this line are merely a bummer,' he thought a little and then shaking his head said, 'Meer qualification does not prove any mettle. Money has an edge over it. Are you ready to go along that way?'

'No, sir,' promptly I said.

'Then prepare for the worst. There is an old proverb: *money makes mare go.*'

'Let the world go its way, but I won't divert my way!'

'Dear, young man, wisdom lies in going along the waves.'

'Then, it will be better to serve a different job.'

'But, you're crossing the age limit for government job?'

'Sir, I won't do any other job except this one.'

'Are you confident to get supporting hand from the so-called stalwarts in this field of education? Will they really, support you?'

'I'm hoping so?'

'Hope is a mere felling or desire of expectation! Hope is like a dangerous hormone that doesn't stimulate the tissues into action. What I mean, hope seldom confers a chance!' he said.

'I agree with your statement, sir,' I confessed.

'Try to do a suitable settlement. It's the only way to get a job in these days. Don't you think so?'

'No, sir, I am determined not do this kind of any settlement. I don't want to be a client to buy a job counting money. Corruptible means I hate deeply.' I frankly opined.

'One should be proud of a man who preserves such principles. I'm glad to meet a boy like you!'

'Guide me the right way, sir?' I asked for his guidance.

'Nothing can be achieved without perseverance, I believe. As you spoke of tolerance, but dare not say to you, my boy?'

'Well, you guide me, sir?'

'Man's condition can aptly be compared to the vacuum cleaners at present. Don't you feel so?'

'Your words are difficult to understand, sir.'

'Why? I'm speaking simple words. Okay, what's your qualification?'

'I'm post-graduate in English Literature and have cleared NET and SET examinations in 2007.'

'Pity! That's a bad thing that a well-qualified young man is still unemployed?'

'Reality, thus, can't be confined.'

'In these depraved and defiled circumstances, one can't hope to torch a light of success and that's pitiful.'

'There is still a kind of impossible chance that I hope for.'

'But my knowledge speaks better. You keep continuing your efforts and hope for the best, but be always prepared for the worst.'

'Right, sir! I'm always. How to alter the worst? That's the problem.'

'I also have gone through all such situations, but never submitted to the odds. *Fight and fight ;Think better*, I adjured every way of my life sincerely,' he added.

'Were you a lecturer?' I asked summing up my daring.

'I've rendered my services as lecturer for twenty-five years and the last eleven years as the principal in one reputable senior college,' he said, clearing his throat.

'Sorry, sir. I beg your pardon for any blemish or unsuitable word I might have spoken to you.'

'No, right now I observed your sincerity. I see an intellectual spark in your eyes. Go along your right way. I wish you will reap success positively one day.'

He filled a kind of thrill into my mind.

He looked as if he had plenty of calculations in his mind, a highly contemplative old man ever had I seen. His expressions showed that he was suffering from some acute disease and was not well in body but feigning to be joyous. It was evident from his body that he must have enjoyed excellent health in his youth and had plenty of money (*he was fond of his wife*). But it was a very pretty thing to note that he was really caught in some sentimental associations (*it is unfair to judge a man from his outward appearance*) and leading life sadly.

'May I know your good name, sir?' I dared asked him.

'What's in the name?' he said and looked at me apathetically.

'That's right, sir!' I apologised.

'Are you the only son to your parents?'

'Right, sir.'

'How do you look for your parents' happiness?'

'It's too good for me to look for my parents' happiness!' I tried to answer his difficult question.

'That's not the answer of my question.'

'I devote time to their services as much as I can,' said I promptly.

'It's because you are still unmarried.'

'After my marriage, I swear to look after my parent's health and happiness.'

'It would be funny if one of these married sons would take care of his old parents!' he smiled secretly.

'Why are you so critical about parents' and sons' relationship, sir?'

'Because, this weak body is also a father of the only son!' he said and cleared his left eye.

'Oh, and daughters?'

'Only son—that's enough!'

'You're too lucky in a real sense.'

'Right! I'm too lucky to squander all my belongings—house, land, bank balance, and pension money—on my only son. I'm too lucky. A man who has lost his dear wife at his fifties; lost his biggest support. Lost his invaluable estate. Lonely life—I'm living a lonely life. Diabetes, high blood pressure, two complicated heart surgeries, and now this weakened eyesight are guarding me. Right boy! I'm too lucky—a father of the only son spending his olden days in *Wriddhhashrama*. But I never surrender to odds—never. Life is a precious gift. So go along—'

He then put his hand into his trousers' pocket to get himself a handkerchief, but then remembering my presence, restrained the gesture and rose up quickly, and saying to me *best luck,* he walked to the parking lanes of the bus stand.

I could not divert my eyes until he disappeared.

Sitting on a bench, I started passing time.

Innumerable thoughts blocked my head.

calculations—chances—almost—bleak—but urgent—to attend—giving up—this way—of—bread *n* butter—so easy—is not—way—*i* must—keep on—attending interviews—not to be—an idle—idle hands—devil's handiwork—idle man—remains idle— must try—possible questions—possible questions—that—can be asked—today—in interview—judge—anticipate—scope of—English literature—vast—vast—too much—bulky—like— to search out—an oyster—into deep waters of ocean—long history—long list of authors—long list of literary works—criticism—much difficult— literary trends—long—long list—my experience— faced—many interviews—experience—enriched— confidence—selection committee members—always ask—limited questions—on—limited topics—on very few authors—ability of candidate—they test—but— who—can test their ability—unnecessarily—kind of revenge—fact is—no candidate—is tested—strictly— all know—fact—appointment—depends upon— bargain—not—on real testing—of knowledge— candidate—remains commodity—purchased—if—you want—policy—market—it is—market—aspirant— commodity—in market—beggar—no choice—beggar like me—travelling with—bag of certificates—scroll of degree—here there anywhere—traveller—fast train—of literature—english literature—vast— bulky—what new—members can ask—can ask— same people—same presidents—same secretaries— same principals same selection committee— same necessity-stricken candidates—same selection procedure—same questions—same results—same winners—same bargain—different amount— money—money—money—acid test—pass through— procedure is procedure—should be followed—what then—leave unwanted matters—concentrate—on questions—preparation—interview—time runs fast— what more—can be asked—shakespeare—milton— dryden—wordsworth—coleridge—shelley—keats— tennyson—browning—modern laureates—joyce or brecht—frost or o'neill—conrad or greene—morrison or gardimer—rushdie or naipaul—tagore or narayan— criticism—fiction—poetry—drama—or—trends *n* grammar—whatever—selectors—masters—ample choice—but—appearing candidate—runs limit—short knowledge—short experience—give *n* take policy— all—in this field—no care—no sympathy—game of money—qualification—least value—laughing stock— disqualification—rules over—corruptible minds—win over—interview—solely a farce—fixing—merely fixing—plays a role— even before—advertisement—to whom—to be avoided—to whom—to be appointed— how much money—be demanded—profit—profit—all's fixed—money-game—business—sheer business— share market—twenty-five—forty lakhs—common rate—for poor—remains dream—people—ready with lakhs—comparison—diversity—what be done—who can stop—who can control—*acchhe din*—*achhe din*—*achhe din*— merits—poor show—quality—poor show—to earn—living—money— problem— seeing is believing—adopt policy—struggle—struggle—even that man—principal—who just—gone—retired— father—of only son—banished king—of his kingdom— sadly said —'m late—but why—how—'m thirty- three—unmarried—young boy—or—middle-aged

man—unemployed—unable—lame—handicapped—
in all respect—*outsider*—camu's *outsider*—fight *n*
fight—think better—he advised—fight—seems lone
word—think—seems weak word—hope—seems
dream—dream—dream of home—dream of wife—
dream of children—dream of two wheeler—dream of
four wheeler—merely dream—*baya weaver*—fine—
hanging nest—nest—intricate texture—beautiful art—
waste of grass-teaks—*baya* weaves—beautiful nest—
my dream home—concrete home—thatched shade—
better home—father—mother—sister *n* sister—*n*
wife—happiness—food—love—affinity—my home—
leave this way—try for business—small one—but—
money—any other work—not possible—contributory
lecturer—short salary—irregular payment—no cycle
even—for travel—daily walk—to reach college—
bus fare—expensive—*mamata*—education—her
fees—mother's illness—her medicines—father's
work— inflation—expenditure—my condition—
my work—smelt of oil—useless—meaningless—
people work—for loaves and fishes—but—'m biting
my lips—licking dust—kneeling down—'m lotus
eater—insulting remark—beating remark—harsh
remark—attack—intolerable—taunting remark—
cut me to quirk—'m always on quiet—no spirit—no
vigour—no aspiration—doomed—intellectual spark—
that principal—seen in me—intellectual spark—
sarita—eulogised me—in me—seen—intellectual
spark—*sarita*—*i will speak*—*thy speech*—*thy love*—
think—*thy thought*—quote—quote of poem—*robert*

browning—poem—*woman's last word*—beautiful poem—*sarita's* last word—her beauty—her smile—her words—her presence—her company—her proposal—terrible dream—terrible dream—dream is dream—oh no—time—great task master—appear for interview—few hours—wait—face interview—try chance— safer side—keep bread *n* butter—try—'m here for—facing interview—try to be—better than others—other candidates—appearing—for interview—that—must—be goal—attitude—be winner—par—care—defeat worries—be confident—be prepared—war ahead—fight—fight—*n* think—better—that—principal advised—so—be confident—you soldier—see your—battle ahead—ahead—ahead—

Think more; think better.

Am I no-hoper? Surely, a nominal person?

But, no! I am zealous and strong in spirit.

My winning and vanquished spirit will fortify my situation? That old man (*the principal*) wished me the success and searched out in me a kind of an intellectual spark.

LONG BUT TO THE POINT,
FAITH IN WORK IS DIVINE.
FROM ALL QUARTERS HIGH,
ROAR FAULTS AND FRAILTIES.

My eyes captured three young girls, who
were seated on the front bench.
A very catchy sight to observe!

Treat everything indifferently without
spoiling by philosophy.
Three young college girls.
All bold, dressed in tight branded
jeans and stylish tops.
Excessively painted faces.
All were playing with their costly
mobile smart-phones.
All looked extravagant.
Trendy.

WORDS THEY SPOKE

'I'm trying, trying and trying—but not connecting,' said the first stylishly.

'Try the second one then? She uses two SIMs always,' said the second in a critical tone.

'Tell number, then?'

'Nine four two—.'

'Ringing? Yes, ring is going.'

'What said; she always keeps close! Very cunning! Very shrewd!'

'Only ring is going *yaar*!'

'Why are you trying then? Won't tell a real reason?' yelled the third.

'Ye! Control your words!' uttered the first again.

'No, she won't disclose?'

'What guarantee? She is a loose-talker?' doubted the second.

'But, very shocking, *yaar*!'

'Why do they all do?' opined the first.

'Madly—blindly!' criticised the third in her rustic style. All three of them were conversing but unhesitatingly.

Open discussion—you may call.

'Study?' started the second, 'won't think it's a case of study?'

'No, no, not at all—some different reasons lie behind such cases—you know?' the first threw a suspicious look around and made her swelling locks neat and pressed her lips with her first finger very stylishly.

The first, a tall and talkative, was a weak but fashionable girl and had a great demonstrative style. The second, a short and showy, was somewhat aged than the three but extraordinarily fidgety. And the third, middle-heighted and harsh, was a thick-bodied and highly pompous girl. All seemed ill-advised and ill-disposed and very bold enough to squander useless words even in the public.

But, what's wrong in it?

It has become a prevalent fashion of talking so proudly on a private life in the public places.

Fashion wins fashion.

'Do you know she squandered fifty thousand rupees on him?' the third opined.

'My god! How then?' enquired the second.

'On Kashmir tour only.'

'Really?'

'No word is false.'

'That's why the elders say love is blind!' the first smiled.

'Love and money go hand in hand. Poor can't afford such *faltu* deeds of love?' the second criticised.

'Right! We're always short of money,' said the third.

'My father send very limited money and I've to manage all expenditures,' the first complained.

'Mine is the same case!' revolted the second.

'My mother always criticises me for not getting admission to engineering degree!' the third grudged.

'After polytechnic diploma, you can seek an admission,' the first suggested.

'No, my mother wants my marriage immediately after clearing diploma.'

'And you?' the second yelled.

'Twenty-two, twenty-three; is it an age of marriage?' the third said.

'All parents want to safeguard their daughters' lives, isn't it?' the second committed.

'Right! But parents become much alert nowadays for their daughters but not for their sons,' the third said.

'My elder brother is running 31 but still enjoying his unmarried life—see!' the first raised her voice.

'My two brothers also married at 30!' the second opened her family secret.

'Marriage, marriage, marriage—all parents rush after daughters only. Sons are all free. See the justice?'

'But, Sushama, I don't find any fault in parents' attitude. They're right!' the second supported the parents.

'See, the life of a girl is not safe even in this twenty-first century,' the first cleared her view.

'Sakshi, are you writing any essay on women's status?' Sushama humorously yelled.

'It's not the matter of humour, Sushama. See, the present condition of women is really worsening day by day.'

'But nobody cares for our young life, our tastes, our joys, our likings, our enjoyments,' Sneha.

'Girls are not born for that,' Sahshi.

SUSHAMA SNEHAL SAKSHI
I came to know their names.

'Sons are emperors!' Sushama.

'Daughters are culprits!' Sakshi.

'Sons are free!' Snehal.

'Daughters are caged birds!'

'Sons have an open sky for a flight!'

'Daughters have to lick the dust.'

'Sons are the kings of nights!'

'Daughters are the prisoners!'

'Sons are made to rape!'

'Daughters are made to suffer!'

'All is free for sons!'

'All is barricaded for daughters!'

'All want sons!'

'Daughters are killed before birth in mother's womb!'

'Law speaks in favour, but nobody acts!'

'And what about suicides?' Sushama opened her mouth in favour of womanhood.

And there, their words ceased for a while.
Short silence ruled over.

'Every daughter is a poor little soul all weep for us!' Snehal tried to divert the course of dialogue.

'This is Indian scenario, Snehal!' Sushama said bluntly.

'On the other hand, the foreign nationals are speaking about surrogacy!' Sakshi put an information.

'Really, that's the progress of the study in human reproductive sciences.'

'*Yeh*, Snehal, have you read something about surrogacy?' Sushma showed her eagerness.

'I've not read much. But little do I know. It is possible for couples to have biologically their own children. It is a method of assisted reproduction through surrogate mothers. Do you know, Sushama, the first surrogate baby was born on June 23rd, 1994. Thereafter, eight years, in 2004, the first surrogate child was born to an Indian woman, and that too in United Kingdom.' Snehal supplied information.

'But, this surrogacy has a very complicated adoption procedure, I think.' Sakshi went on.

'Is it free for a willing woman to enter the procedure of surrogacy?' Sushama asked.

'I've not clear knowledge about this, but I've read somewhere that a woman who is willing to enter this surrogacy must attain the age between 21 and 35 years and she also has to enter into a legally enforceable surrogacy agreement.'

'And we are still hesitating to accept inter-caste marriages!' Sushama grudged.

'Only talking about inter-religious marriages!'

'Indians have the habit of talking; seldom accept acting!'

'Good comment!'

All three were discussing.

FRANK DISCUSSION

But a kind of hesitation and dubious
suspicion was reigning over their mind.

'Sad, sad, sad! Snehal, we're speaking about that Neha?'
Sakshi reminded the opening of a dialogue.
'Yeh! Neha's case!'
'My god! How and why she opened all her cards so
easily?' Sushama added.
'Simple looking, but she was vainglorious.'
'*Arrey*, this is the matter of fifty thousand only, yet she
spent much more on him.'
'You know all secrets then?'
'If this be true, what way that boy is wrong?'
'Overtly, how simple looking she was!' Sakshi.
'*Yaar*, outward appearance is always deceptive!' Snehal.
'Hum, really—fine faces are always deceptive—right!'
Sushama.
'Only of our age you know?'
'Yes, more or less the same of our age.'
'Why then this much haste for marriage?'
'What else she could do? He played all the plans—
shrewdly caught her and deceived!'
'But had she been so small a child—really not knowing
anything about him?'
'Blind, *yaar*, love is blind!'

Sushama uttered the word *love* so carefully
that nobody could sense a doubt even.
Then they came on the real track and
began speaking in a repressed tone.

'What a tragedy?' Sushama.

'Time never waits and watches. I won't say it's a tragedy!' Sakshi.

'Bad luck. What else?' Snehal.

'She could have saved her if she could have waited. No bad luck.'

'Think so?'

'Okay! But, why should only a girl meet the punishment like this? Why not the boys—when they themselves activate all these situations. Play their games and leave the girls for suffering. Suicide is only meant for a girl in such situations.'

'Take care. People might be watching our words?' Snehal cautiously threw a glance around.

'People haven't a work either but to poke nose into the others' matters,' Sakshi revolted.

All three became cautious.

They became suspicious, but they were bold
enough to discuss such issues in the public.

Ladies cannot control words when they are in a group. Grouped ladies are always aggressive or corroborative, highly under the impact of the actors in daily soaps.

'She was trapped by that boy,' Sakshi continued.

'Two years continuously he played with her and left in the throes,' Snehal criticised.

'Tantalised and deceived,' Sushama grieved.

'Had she been known to all his plans? Might be in a doubt?' convulsed Snehal.

'If such things happen, nobody believes anybody! And I think, Snehal, he knew it well that she was rich. Her father and mother both earn handsome salary. Very good acres of land, bank balance, flats, residential bungalow, top class car, servants at door—rich indeed! Cunningly trapped her,' Sakshi added information.

'How cunning he is!' exclaimed Sushama.

'She wanted to marry him by sacrificing her studies. Quite bewildered—even then?' Snehal.

'*Saala badmash!* It was his plan of exploiting money. Was not interested in marriage! What such boys have to do with marriage and life of the girls? They're like hunters who run after always keeping eyes on preys.'

'Sakshi! Control yourself. Take care,' Snehal attributed.

'Oh, no! My matter is different. I don't fall a prey to such insanity.'

'It's all the game of money. Bloody who has money to ride on such a dark horse?'

'Silent! Silent! Walls also have ears!' Sushama warned.

'But don't you think, Snehal, that we all shouldn't surrender ourselves to such mad situations?' Sakshi.

'Instead, we should fight and teach a lesson to such rascal boys. Why should we fall a prey to their libidinous desires? *Matalabi saaley!* Actually, Neha was not so bad a girl. She was derring-do. She wasn't a girl to submit to such a situation so easily.' Snehal attacked her views.

'Ha *yaar*, might be some serious reason behind it?'

'Guess?'

'What else?'

'At least, your guess?'

'Pregnancy!'

'And resulted suicide?'

'My god! Pity!'

All three stopped.
All started looking at each other.
Silent! Quiet! Dumb!
Oh! serious matter—but gewgaw was it actually!

SECRET WAS DISCLOSED
WOMAN SUFFERS A LOSS OF APPETITE

SUICIDE

Disconcerted, I looked around; the crowd
being swollen kept me unstable.
My head kept on paining. Wakefulness
had reddened my eyes.
Exerted feeling made me restless.
suicide—suicide—word suicide—became—prevalent
like fashion—girls—committing suicide—for
unwanted—reasons—rapes—common—boys—
turning—culprits—killers—rapists—kidnappers—
girls—suffer—problem—fall to—boys' deceptive—
promises—allurement—lures—baits—pregnancy—
curse—before marriage—welcoming—after
marriage—karuna—motiram sawkar's—only
daughter—committed—suicide—pregnancy—
carried her—to commit—suicide—just yesterday—
had read—terrible news—of rape—and—my god—
school-going boy—burnt girl—alive—after rape—one
collegian—young boy—killed—his father—for—want

of—merely—thousand rupees—is it—tendency—or—
perversity—mulishness—intransigence—under—
impact—of films—daily-soaps—rape scenes—
galore—cruelty-loaded scenes—youth—both—sex—is
victimised—one article—writes—testosterone level—
makes man—more aggressive—to committing—
crimes—women are—more likely—to be—psychotic—
crime is crime—crime against body—crime against
property—crime against—public order—crime
against women—crime against children—cruelty by—
husbands and relatives—increasing—day by day—new
born deaths—accounting greatly—about 40 per cent—
over—violent crimes—ruin lives—ruin harmony—
aggressive—horrible—cognisable crimes—and
youth—falls prey—to such crimes—prisons full—
cheating and counterfeiting—common—kidnapping—
raping—abduction—cancerous growth—number of—
new born babes—in—this land—is highest—in the
world—new born—babe—*maya*—hardly lived—for
year—her—husband—exploited money—from—
father—left her—alone—to suffer—doubt—she is—
big with—young—young—young—

*May heat was at the peak. And the life gasped worst.
Scarcity of drinking water made the people to run
down the small river and search out the water anyhow
by digging in the small ditches into the soil-land of
the river and fetching water from a long distance. A
hectic schedule right from the early hours of morning
to the scorching heat hours of the day and again the*

second round up to the dark hours of evening. Usual but inevitable scene in the region. For fetching water, I was in the queue carrying two big buckets in my hands. It took me an hour to come back home. It was Sunday and no any other work was spared for me except to look after my mother and help my father into the field. I prepared meal. My younger sister had gone to the field with my father. My mother was resting. She was suffering from severe cough and catarrh. My father had to come back from the field. My mother needed an urgent and good medical treatment. I had requested my college principal yesterday to release my outstanding salary but he had cited some inexcusable reasons for the deposit of salary. Wherefrom the money be collected? Overburdened already of having forty thousand rupees lending on the head! Engrossed in cared thoughts, I sat on the floor and took an old newspaper and the news on the front page at once captured my attention: 'a married girl set on fire by her husband.'

Very shocking news it was!

Suddenly, a crying-voice stunned my ears, and I saw my elder sister coming slowly with some trouble in her legs like a toddler and covering her face with a pallu of sari. I walked to her and took her inside the home. She came and began to weep heavily. I gave her a glass of water but she broke loose. Her reddened eyes and scattered hair, tattered sari, and flattered body were enough to tell the story of her worsened condition. She wept and wept and wept. My mother came down from her bed and asked her in a stuttering sound,

'Maya, Maya, why are you here in this condition?' She fell on the mother's chest and wept heavily. She was frightened like a wounded deer. Only her cries could demonstrate her agonised condition? And she couldn't hide her agony as it was very severely imprinted on her body.

I asked her calmly, 'What's the matter sister, tell me?'

'Can't live with him hereafter?' she said and sobbed.

'That's apparent from your condition,' said I and looked carefully at her. A few marks of burning could be seen very clearly on her face. I understood the happening. And in soft voice again I asked, 'Is he so brutal and for what?'

'For money,' she said.

'For money?'

'Humm!'

'Last month, he took two thousand rupees from me?'

'Don't know, but he asked ten thousand more.'

'Ten thousand?' exclaimed I.

'And what about the money given as dowry?'

'All spent on trivial dealings.'

'Tell me the truth, he works really or just befooling all?' I asked suspiciously.

'From the last six months he is vacant, and drinks heavily, wanders with his bastard friends, and does nothing except eating meals and dinners at home—' clearing tears from her eyes, she said.

'And what happens to your joining?'

'No, nothing happened more important. He squandered all money and didn't pay even a pie to the bargainers as it was bargained. I'm vacant.'

'But you had said last month that you've joined the school, you know?'

'Yes, because of his threat?'

'My god! Slipped away the golden chance? Service is not so easy. Who can tell?'

'He and his family members have no value of education instead they opt to work in routine housing works.'

'Mistake is made. Hastily taken decision,' I opined repentance.

'Don't do anything more now. I won't go back to his home. I'll leave him. And if I don't, he will take my life— so mad he is?' and Maya spread her body on the floor.

'Don't worry and don't be so panicky. Remember I'm here for you,' said I vigorously.

'No, no, Dada, no! Don't take a risk? Don't throw money on his stake? I won't go back. Suicide—only suicide can save my—, ' and I blocked her words in her mouth by closing her lips.

'Maya, don't speak more—don't speak. Have you lost your courage so easily—and for this trivial matter? No, Maya, don't submit to the dangers so easily.' I backed a ray of hope in her heart.

A big problem had to be faced.

I was caught in a critical condition from all sides. My father had to solely work harder to meet both ends and had no income as the monsoon went dry and no crop helped. Only one year had gone for her marriage *and my father had spent seventy thousand rupees on marriage, a bigger amount of forty thousand rupees had been spent on dowry. All conditions of the bridegroom party had been accepted and fulfilled even before the marriage. And the boy was jobless—no permanent job—working on daily wages. He had asked money for getting a permanent job. But the truth was very different. It increased my responsibility towards my sister, increased my inability in making her suffer, but it would have been better to settle her married life by this or that way. But how?*

My father came back home.

'It is awful to hear it?' he said dimly.

I didn't know what to say.

Minutes passed by in grave silence.

'Maya tried to adjust, but it passed beyond her tolerance,' said my mother.

'There's no reason why should that bastard give her trouble.'

'My daughter's fate,' my mother said sadly.

'I knew not well enough the reality and, thus, made the decision. I wasted my girl. I myself am responsible for her suffering,' he spoke with a kind of gasp.

'Fate rules over every human being!'

'You can say so, but I can't?'

'How to speak the truth, a problem?' mother stammered.

'I'm so ready to hear any truth and that's my fate!' Father gave an angry look at the sky.

'I don't think you'll like the truth if it is disclosed to you,' she said and observed his face.

'My condition is like a reformed drunkard, tell you and
I've got the best mind to suffer any hard blow—so, don't
worry; disclose it.'

She remained silent for a while.

Maya rushed madly into the laps of her father and,
confining her face, started weeping heavily.

Looking at Maya sadly, I imagined a deserted,
abandoned life of a married sister.

My father controlled his emotions with his ablest
skill and tried to pacify the gravity of situation.

'I'm sorry, child, I made a mistake. I am as shocked by
the punishment imprinted on your face and back as if
I see that rascal beating you in the public. That giant
doesn't know any kind of endearment supposed to be
entrusted to a woman—his wife. But I've to teach him
a lesson. I just want to know where is he.'

My father's face, almost robust in its
severity and gauntness, softened.

He affectionately put his hand on Maya's head
and imprinted elegant kisses on her shoulders.

But he tried to hide his tears gathered in his eyes.
Acute lassitude blackened his face but he exerted an
attempt not to exude the torturing pains in his heart.

My mother fomented that ugly situation as if she
was ready to punish that rascal seriously.

Mamata, my younger sister, tried to
shy off the sorrows of situation.

I turned pale.

The wind howled outside.

It was the hottest day.

My heart became very anxious to
know the fact of that happening.
I was feeling as if somebody injected a poison into
my veins. My anxious heart was eating up my body.
Silence ruled over the home.
Suddenly, there came a sound of footsteps at the door.

'Anjani? Anjani?' the voice came and Gangubai,
an old woman, poked her head round the door and slunk
back and after a while entered home unhesitatingly.
A kind of darkness was spread over every corner of
the home even in the bright daylight. All of us became
cautious on her sudden arrival. Gangubai shrugged
her shoulders in her shanty style and cleaned a sweat
on her forehead by a tattered corner of lugada.

She looked quite secretly at us and said, 'I never
could have dared to have a nap in the hotter day like
this. Hot, hot, very hot! Glasses of water I drank, but,
Anjani, wol you give me glass of cold water? My throat
burning!' and she sat close to Mamata on the floor.

She did look dashed! A dastard old woman!
She drank a glass of cold water.
Her arrival was purposeful.
Gangubai, mother of five daughters and two sons, had
a hard life. Her misery was so terrible that she had lost
her husband after the birth of her last son. She worked
hard for family. But inborn crafty nature made her
infamous in the village. She was a figure of scorn.
'Arrey! Maya's here? When did you come, Maya?' she
asked.
'Today only!' Maya adjusted her words skilfully.

'Maya, you do look tired, you do!' she spied her little eyes on Maya's face.

'No!'

'Are you alone?'

'Yeh!'

'And how's your mother-in-law?'

'Well!'

'And my son-in-law?'

'Well!'

'Wot is it, you err here?' she asked.

'Here? For no special work?' Maya replied.

    She then scraped her one ear with her middle
          finger and looked closely at Maya.

'Owe, are you coming for mango-ras dinner tonight? Don' you?' she asked.

    Every moment, my mother grew restless and
        my father flung a kind of rage on his face.

'So hotter a day, today! She just came,' my mother interrupted Gangubai's words.

'My god! Alone on such a hot day?' She enlarged her suspicious eyes.

    She looked, eyes wide apart, at Maya's stomach.
             SILENCE
    How strong and strange suspicion
      was swelling into her eyes!
  Her unwanted presence made me turbulent really!
    I was about to speak; I held my tongue.
Suddenly, there came a screech of motorcycle outside.
   Swirling the key chain in style, he appeared at
    the door as if tumbled from the motorcycle.

'Where is she, my wife?' he spoke. 'Why should she be
here?'

My father quickly came to the door.
I too. My mother rose up and held
Maya's hand. Mamata helped her.
Reaching the top of the doubt, Gangubai
fixed her eyes on the outsider.

'Err you here?' Gangubai exclaimed.

'Give me the way inside,' he said.

'Come, come,' she said and drew back.

'Where is my wife?' he growled.

'Come inside,' my father said politely.

'No, I'm not here to sit and rest. I'm in hurry.'

There was no need of evidence
that he was heavily drunk.

'I won't ask you to rest. But hear me a little?' said my
father again.

'No! It makes such loose wife so silly a thing—leaving
her husband's home!' he scathed his words.

Highly tormented by fear, Maya held father's hand
and cried, 'No, no, father, I won't go with him!'
I could not resist myself.

'Say clearly, what you have to—?' I stood before him.

He zonked.

He was not in a condition to speak clearly.
A heavy dose of desi daru had
made him so flapdoodle.

'Leave that matter with me, man! I want my wife with
me?' he zonked again.

'She is not here?' I said and hinted Maya to go in the dinette.

'Owe, you son of a pig; I'll kick you out. Go out! Go out of my sight! Says I? Owe, she is not here?' he growled again.

'You're not in a sense now. How dare you enter my home in this condition?' my father rebuked.

Gangubai laughed execrably.

My mother flapped like a wounded bird.

'It's my right, owe, man! It's my right! I'm here in my wife's home? Woo are you to bark like a stray dog?' he clamoured.

Highly distasteful look of Gangubai
made the scene more ghastly.

'This tamasha is not good. Say what are you here for?' my father tried to pacify him.

'Tamasha? Owe, man! This is not tamasha!' he broke his nasty words loose. 'This is a real film. Husband and wife love shhtorey! Don't play villain yourself! Kill you. Not even a trailer! My love shhtorey, understand? I want my wife. I'll take her my home.'

Then in a severe feat of drunkenness, he stroke
his head against the wall and laughed madly.

A man of a dead soul!

And Gangubai smiled beastly.

That afternoon had been awful!

He then turned back and pulled up his shirt and aired up his nostrils. He coughed up mucus severely. Trembling with anger, that bastard kicked an empty glass on the floor and stared at my mother in the face.

'Call your daughter soon and pocket me twenty thousand rupees early. No time to waste. Damn pigs— nonsense! Get me money and let me go. Where's that my dear wife? Owe, are you there? Come—let's go! Brought a horse for you deeerr, see, see, outside—that horse is waiting for us! Come, come—dear come—' he accosted and again kicked a glass.

We all became cautious.

Gangubai whimpered deliberately!

Firmly, I came to him and affirmed, 'No money and no wife. Get out. Don't show your face again?'

In return, he took out a knife from his trousers' pocket and, aiming at me, growled 'Owe, don't dare! I'll kill you!'

Suddenly, Maya came out from dinette and she stood before him and roared, 'How dare you touch my brother, you rascal?'

He had not moved an inch. He stood very still.

'Be right back! There is no anything that you want here? And don't show your power to my brother? Keep your mind going and run back your way,' Maya said mercilessly.

He retreated a step and said, 'I'll need you to go back home.'

Maya was firm on her decision.

PRICELESS IS THY LOVE, O SISTER!
WHO CAN FATHOM ITS DEPTH?
THY HEART IS A BLISSFUL OYSTER!

WHERE DWELLS A LOVE ADEPT.

Outside rain clouds blackened the sky more lavishly.
Rain might tighten its jack. Rain!
Rain! Rain! Unseasonable!
It came late this year and strolled its way.
It's life and it's death for farmers.

My mind went back home.
Dismal! Despicable! Numb!

—mother—my mother—also tired—my mother—
looks more aged—than she really is—excessive work—
excessive burden—excessive anxiety—excessive
care—made her—much older—my mother— real
example of—an ideal—workmanship *n* dutifulness—
my goddess—my spirit—my life—my estate—corners
of home—silent—summarisation—of pangs—
pathos—great novels—plays—seem blunt—situation
of—my home—seemingly pale—no comparison—
before it—no gravity—at all—all those stories—not
even—*anton chekhov's—the antagonist*—narration—
summarisation—all useless—faint before it—but—this
restlessness—this dejection—this doldrums—can't—
let me—breathe—while—head cracking—mind
gobbling—body aching—doing nothing—sitting—
knowing—how—take—step ahead—what way—
be gone—what decision—be taken—all chaos—in
mind—problem of—getting rid of—confusion—
confusion—confusion—still—have to—kill

time—two hours—wait—two more hours—walking distance—just two kilometres—from here—reach college—on time—why care—no botheration—few minutes—walking distance—but—rain—rain—yes—rain—main problem—how—can be—over there—if—rain continues—no care—for clothes—no care—for body—but—certificates—no—protective bag even—certificates—oh—no—certificates—my bread—my butter—my bread—my salt—bred *n* butter—bread *n* salt— whole family—father's dream—mother's hope—sisters' protection—divorcee sister—my sweat—my accomplishment—certificates—matriculation—degree—post-graduate—net—set—certificates—all—priceless—invaluable—my estate—my property—my belongings—oh— no—care—be taken—be—saved all—dampening—damaging—can't believe—can't imagine—be saved all—see—observe—crowd—crowd—crowd—people—people—people—crowd—everywhere— rush—chaos—everywhere—no peace—no silence—largest democracy—this nation—land of people—land of population—*i'm*—neglected citizen—of—great land—neglected—oh—yes—of course—neglected—neglected—what sense—why—neglected—meaningless—why should—submit to—circumstances—so easily—why should—surrender to difficulties—odds—no—not—way—should not—by any cost—recollect—*ulysses*—words—strive—struggle—but—not to yield—see—life—become—hard—afflicting—unemployment—inflation—corruption—debauchery—violence—deviated—

troubled—pathless—worsening life—unstoppable—limitless—irreparable—uncontrollable—diseases—hypertension—diabetes—arthritis—cancer—aids—medicines—injections—life—thoughts—thoughts—thoughts—father—hard worker—growing old—weakening body—under burden—under tension—but hopeful—strong warrior—strong combatant—good acumen—wants—son—daughter—all educated—stresses—on—education—loves learning—dared—care taker—helping—his aspiration—is hope—rests on—on his—only son—but—still unemployed—long for—a job—crave for—principles—what is—important— principle—or—bread *n* butter—problem—must—must—a job is—must—save—bread *n* butter—my—bread *n* butter—

The wall clock of the bus-station showed eleven.
The huge crowd was then at the peak.
Killing of time also had become a great task for me!
Earnestly, I rose from my place and eagerly
walked towards the book stall.

I had no extra money to buy even a newspaper, but could not resist myself to see the lavishly printed covers of some magazines of my choice and I stood at the counter of the bookstore. Under a genuine feat of curiosity, I touched one new magazine and, holding it on from the stand, began to turn over the pages, but the shopkeeper shouted in a robust tone, '*Oye*, 've to purchase—no ? Put it. Keep it down.' Awakened, I felt sorry and just stood before the stand rolling my eyes on the stock of books and magazines and newspapers shyly. The October issue of *Outlook* was fairly good. Reading had been my passion since my secondary school days; reading of Ramayana and Mahabharata, Shivpurana and Navnatha Mahima Kathasar, Isapniti, Vinoba Bhave, Premchand, Rabindranath Tagore, Somerset Maugham, Katherine Mansfield, Jawaharlal Nehru, Nirad C Chaudhary, Mahadevi Verma were my lovable writers. A good habit of reading made me too strong in reading section to seek more and more reading options, right from mythology, astrology, science, fiction to history. In that sense, I was an adept reader—to a little degree voracious reader. In addition, I was little bit a good writer. I tried more to publish, but only a fraction touched the hearts of publishers; saddened to think quite inexperienced in the field of writing.

A hanky-panky feeling of touching the book sans
bookseller's permission hankered my inner urge.
Hushing sorry for the deed, I neared back again
to the bench where I sat before a few minutes.
But the place was occupied by
one strong young fellow.
I stood just by the side of the bench.
A young boy on the bench was tall, fair, strong, and smart—his eyes big and black, his face covered up with black beard, and he looked fresh and energetic like a blossom of cotton flower.
He glanced at me.

I smiled.

He courtly said, 'Please, sit here!'
         And he paced a seating place for me.
                  He seemed quite affable.
'Thanks,' said I and sat beside him.
'Relax. Don't mind!' he said politely.
'The rain came so unexpectedly that it thumped the farmers' hearts at throes,' I tried to make him speak.
'Delayed occurrence of it, is also a welcoming fact. So no grudge!' he said.
'Don't you think this weather is changing day by day?' I opened discussion without knowing his taste for it.
'What do you understand by *weather*?' he asked me stressing the word *weather*.
'It is the state of the *atmosphere* at a place and time,' I replied.
'Referring to the side from which the wind is blowing, okay!' he completed my statement.
'Right, brother!'
'And what do you understand by *atmosphere*?' he asked.
    His curious look made me to think on the term.
'Can't produce a scientific definition, but simply can say, *atmosphere* is related to air, gas, and temperature surrounding the earth.'
         I tried to define the word *atmosphere*.
'Scientifically, atmosphere is a word of two Greek origins: *atmos* means *vapour* and *sphaira* means *globe*; so it is the quality of air surrounding the earth—to my little knowledge,' said he.

'Right, brother!' I praised.

From his words, I learned that he was
a qualified young boy of my age.

'So what do you think, who is responsible for this change in *atmosphere*?' he questioned.

'A great deal of reasons are responsible for this?' I replied.

'What are the prominent reasons?'

'Pollution, may be the first one?' I said hesitatingly.

'And who is responsible for pollution?'

'Of course, the man is responsible for all this pollution?'

'So, why do you blame the *nature*?'

'No, I don't blame the *nature*?'

'So you said, the rain came so unexpectedly?' he wanted to clarify my words.

'Excuse me, brother!'

'*Unexpected* always is an excuse when nothing comes to us *expectedly*—so it is!'

'Right, brother!'

'So it is unwise to blame *nature*?'

'Right?'

'What are you doing nowadays?'

'I am searching a job.'

'Search of a job is also a great change in the present employment system, am I correct?'

'Right, brother!'

'What job?' he asked briefly.

'Lecturer's?' I replied briefly.

'Much difficult job to search for?'

'Are you employed, brother?' my curiosity arose.

'No, I don't believe in employment.'

'Why?'

'It's a sheer waste of time and money, I firmly believe.'

'What one can do when he possesses requisites for the job?'

'Mere requisites can't work in this present employment system? It needs other demoralised sources.'

'Man's doggedness is testifying here?'

'Doggedness, determination, resolution, persistence, obduracy, endurance, all are weak words when we speak of employment and a barefooted man has to endure the baleful wound of a thorn; a qualified man has to suffer a long blow of time. Every man is bamboozled by timely changes and occurrences. I never think desperately, but this side of employment is really muddling and mind-gobbling,' he said in an acute desperation.

'Since last six years I'm searching a job?' with a slight hesitation, I opened my secret.

'Six years is a long period.'

'Yes, I know?'

'Every year, month, week, and day is valuable in man's life and you said of six years. Pity!'

'There is no other go?'

'Ways are to be searched for? How do you earn for a living?' he asked me a straight question.

'I serve as contributory lecturer in one college.'

'How much do you get for this waste of time?'

'Hardly, twelve to thirteen thousand a year?'

'Approximately, one thousand a month?'

'Right, brother.'

'The worth of one thousand you know very well—right?'

'Right, brother.'

'And I earn minimum ten to twenty lacks per annum.'

'Fine, brother!'

'Won't you ask me how do I earn such a big amount?'

'How, brother?' I asked in strange curiosity.

'From agricultural production. I own only fifteen acres of land, but I work day in and day out and use all scientific methods for cultivation and production relying not upon traditional methods of agriculture and the changing moods of weather. I always get myself ready to accept and endure any climatic change— weather's burst or bliss—whatever. After all man has no control over all these natural occurrences; that man has to presuppose and has to work accordingly,' he explained.

'Are you a graduate in agriculture?' acute curiosity made me to ask him about his qualification.

'Right, brother! I'm M Sc in agriculture, and visited two countries for agricultural studies so far. I tried hard to bring my agricultural set up and now it is on the well go,' he said.

Then he looked at the bustling crowd at the bus station.

There rose a respect for him in the corner of my heart. He preferred the solid life to the wasting employed life. In a little time, I learnt very much from his mutual acquaintance, and I could not help feeling a little surprised, even shocked, that he adopted a solid way of life not submitting to the outcries of tainted ways. He infused a kind of spirit into my heart and awakened me. 'Why then people of our region commit suicide?' I asked sharply.

'Suicide is a deliberate act to finish life, I suppose,' he cleared his opinion.

'Right, but why this deliberate and deleterious act which is extremely damaging to one's own interests?'

'When we say *deliberate*: the meaning is crystal clear.'

'I look sadly at this happening. It has become a common business now to end life. Sad and sad and sad!'

'Emotional attitude to life is always sad as you believe in sad and sad and sad—and like this!'

'But, why farmers only?'

'Because farmers have deprecated their hopes for life and accepted depredations losing spirit to fight out?'

'Just now I have read the news on the front page of a newspaper: *two more farmers commit suicide*,' I supported my information.

'It has become a daily business and nobody is ready to curate these muddling minds; if it is a problem,' he continued, 'High debt burdens, mansoon failure, and government policy are cited the sole reasons; but a very few talks of personal issues and family problems?'

'Failure of cash crops is the prominent reason, but family problems also are increasing day by day.'

'There may be a gigantic bunch of problems; debt, alcohol addiction, chronic disease, private money lenders, stress of family responsibilities, increased cost of cultivation can also be added to all these problems.'

He had a long strange smile on his dark-bearded face.
He appeared neither offended nor
shocked by the news of suicide.
He then took a pen of his shirt's pocket.
Taking out one diary from his *paijama*'s pocket,
he started noting down something in English.
Might be some important matter he had
forgotten or might be a casual buying matter!
Minutes passed by.
Crowd grew bigger and shouts grew louder.

'Farmers must be saved from this agonising deed,' I continued the talk again.

'Saving is in one's own hands; others can't do anything for saving,' he said sadly.

'Right, brother, but some remedies may work upon this problem.'

'On deliberate acts, one should find his own remedies; he must be the saviour of his own!'

'Four months ago, one hard-working farmer of my village committed suicide.'

'Did you find out the reasons for it?'

'Reasons for it are unknown yet, but some people speak of the bank loans as the sole reason behind it!'

'Why do you say *unknown*?' he pelted a doubt.

'Really, the actual reason is not yet known to anybody?' I cleared my point.

'*Known* and *unknown* are merely the play of words. Reasons are very clear. I may be wrong, but I think man has lost his faith in work. Man wants everything easy and fast. Patience and perseverance are rarely found in this farming generation. Remember, every man should be solid in mind. Nature is changing and this change must be accepted. But, man should think of the other side of a life. Ways are many, but we barricaded all. Open the ways and lead the life—*a mantra for success, happiness,*' he continued promptly. 'I always think on my fellow farmers' suicidal attempts but sorry to say that the reasons behind their suicides are sometimes so normal that I wonder why do they accept death instead of fighting against problems and situations. After all, committing suicide is a hard mind's work.'

He then took a deep breath.

A streak of high confidence blazoned his face.

'I appreciate your knowledge and understanding,' I praised.

'Both are the fruits of time,' he said and smiled.

'Time is precious, I understand, but baffle to know why it takes revenge against some of us.'

'Time never takes revenge against anybody. Many of us do not understand the value of time. I know many factors may be responsible for keeping abreast of time, but how many of us are able to settle that time in a right pace?'

'You may be right!'

'Time always tests the man?'

'Right! Brother, say your opinion on global warming?' I eagerly asked him.

'Global warming! See, it's a big topic for discussion. Very difficult to understand!' he said.

'But, it is said that this bigger climate change is because of global warming?'

'Right. Mainly, global warming is caused by rising levels of carbon dioxide in the atmosphere. These levels make a dark blanket and act to contain radiated heat. This increased heat raises overall temperatures to very dangerous levels. Melting of snow, rise in sea levels, causing much disturbance to the land. It resulted into unpredictable weather and changing climate patterns,' he recited the information.

'What are the positives and negatives of this global warming?'

'Oh, brother, rightly you're testing my knowledge!' he smilingly remarked.

'No, brother! No, this is not a testing in any way? My curiosity urged me to ask—that's why?' I said politely.

'Environmental pollution: such as air pollution, water pollution, radioactive pollution, soil pollution, deforestation, is making a serious problem. The scientists say that approximately 20 to 30 per cent of species are likely to be at increased risk of extinction if warming exceeds 1.5 to 2.5 degrees Celsius. See, what danger may come upon the earth!' he explained.

'Yesterday, I had read one term related to the culture of agriculture in one current magazine. Not recollecting properly now.'

'You may be saying about *permaculture*—right?' he rightly pointed out a term.

'Right! Right! That's that term.'

'*Permaculture* is a combination of permanent culture and agriculture. It is basically about ensuring that the earth's limited resources are used in equitable and wise ways,' he rightly supplied the information.

Then there rose a big sound of
quarrel between two men.
That broke our discussion.

'Come on, we will have a cup of tea?' he smiled and asked me to follow him.

'No. it's okay!' I said.

'Oh, come on friend. A cup of tea is also enough to shatter the tension in such dubious condition and you're going on a war—I mean your interview. Right? So, come on. Shake off hesitance!' He rose from his place.

I enjoyed a tea with him.

Wishing me a success wholeheartedly, he went out of the bus station.

His exit shoved me into the dell of
my best friend's domain.

NOVEMBER 2007

Dr Kane's hospital was jam-packed with patients.
Severe catarrh foxed me to list my
name in the waiting patients.
Waiting went on for half an hour.
But I couldn't wait more as my
examination was over my head.
Decidedly, I made my way back to the
bus station to catch the bus.

Complete one and a half hours was wasted on travel.
On reaching home, I directly joined my study.
The revision of the Romantic Period was my target for
the day. Anyhow, it had to be completed by evening as
the examination was just a week ahead. Wish for a cup
of tea disturbed me for a while, but I suppressed it. It
was all very bad for me that day, as I had had no meal
for the previous night, and being fond of ginger tea, it
was very difficult to repress the demand of mind. I felt
as if I was languishing in jail. But I determined to go
with my study and even passing it on to burn midnight
oil. Only Mamta was at home. All others had gone out
to the field. Silence ruled over every nook and corner
of the home.
Sudden ominous barking of a dog followed by
a gentle knock on the door arrested my ears.
The knocking came in a burst.
I walked to the door and opened it.
He was Hemant!
I was astounded by his unexpected
presence at my door.
Hemant rushed in, having taken a deep breath,
he sat on my cot and got relaxed as if he was coming from
a long journey. His wearisome face had been describing
some worrisome happening rather suspicious.
Mamta gave him a glass of water.
Hemant scraped his right ear with his
finger and looked around nervously.
The boy, who had been a live wire for me, was looking
intensely worried and disturbed. The boy, who had so

much interest and speculation centred on him, was that day on the point of distraction of spirit. Looking anxiously in all directions, he gave a few random gestures and sighed again. His face was variously masked with indifference, ghastly pallor, and blazing with defiance. It seemed as if he was heading for the hills. Never had I seen him in such a chaotic condition.
'You're looking nervous today?' I asked him apprehensively.

'Can you spare some time for me, please?' he asked.
Then we travelled the road on the motorcycle.
A twenty minutes ride brought us to his farm.
On reaching there, Suresh, his faithful servant, welcomed us saying, 'Come, maalak!'
We sat under the shadow of a mango tree.
'What made you bring me here?' I asked him worriedly.
'Nothing? I wanted to have a talk with you; no other special reason,' he said calmly.
'Hemu, I know you better. Say clearly?' I complained.
'That's why you're here!'
'What is it exactly that you're worried about?' I tried to read his face.
'I'm not worried; I'm baffled,' he said.
'By what?'
'By life!
'Hemu, you know better than me what life is?' I stressed.
'No, you're wrong!'
'Why are you so penitentially sad today?'
'Because, sadness is an essence of Hemant's life!'

'I disagree with your view, rightly,' I tried to pull him out of that situation.

'Don't you think, Ajju, that the mental and emotional climate we're living in affect our life?' he questioned.

'Hemu, you're a powerful thinker, indeed!'

'But, you're a scholar.'

'Don't compare my tiny scholarship with your high grade thinking,' I said.

A vagrant, deep flush flowed into his forehead.

He was looking away from him at the far downing sky.

I felt, suddenly, horribly tired.

He was but enfolded in that strange,

strong, suspicious situation.

'Ajju, to what extent the term luck is a true entity?' he asked.

'Luck is a secondary occurrence in man's life!' I stated.

'And what's primary?'

'Man's work.'

'Mere work would make man's life?'

'Of course, it would!'

'And, then, what about this mental and emotional climate?'

'Hemu, why do you stress on the word "climate"?'

'Because climate plays an important role in man's life.'

'Are you pondering on some character to be added to your new writing?'

'No, I myself am that character.'

'In my opinion, more powerful is economical climate,' I authentically opined.

The day was quite sunny.
Suresh brought a tray of tea and said, 'Sip this
ginger tea, Malaak. You both look unwell.'
While sipping tea, I looked carefully at his face.
His nonchalant face reflected more
and more strange pangs!
And then there sounded a sonorous cooing of
koel through the dense leaves of mango tree.

'See, this is what I understand as "climate". Lovely, it's simply melodious!' Hemu excitedly exclaimed.

'Only a poet's mind can fathom its depth; can hunt for such mysterious meaning!' I forwarded my view.

'Ajju, can you gather the meaning of this cooing of koel?' he asked.

Looking up into the dark bush of mango tree, he smiled and threw a small stone at the birds flying in the sky.

STRANGE STRANGE STRANGE

His behaviour grew confused to me.
He, then, gave a little smile, stifling a cry of surprise.
I made no reply to his question.

'Ajju, don't dumb your tongue. Say something,' he continued.

'Hemu, you're a great watcher of birds, so only you can gather the meaning from such cooing.'

'Have you read that poem by Wordsworth named "To the Cuckoo"?'

'Yeh!'

'That koel is hallooing his mate too amorously to attract her, you know!' he smiled secretly.

'Only a man who knows ornithology can understand this.'

'I'm probably more aware of the mental and emotional climate!' he repeated the same word 'climate'.

'There is no end to such discussion,' I wanted to close his words.

'No, everything has an end!'

'Unfortunately, we're badly misconstrued and misperceived people?'

'We're the people in disguise. Aren't we the dogs wearing democratic suits?'

He made a vehement attack on man's status.

Why was he so critical saying tragic words!

'All of us have several needs and wants and everyone is running after to satisfy them eagerly,' said I.

'Every human being is always and ever hungry or thirsty for one thing?'

'But, if it's so, you must master the art of catering to the perennial hunger?'

'That's right?' he alluded positively.

'May I quote one story?' I asked.

'Of course, you can. You're a great tale-teller. Go on,' he turned to me.

Narration of the story went on.

'Carrying a small hammer in her cracked and wrinkled hands, she sits in the midst of rust. She is painstakingly busy in cleaning the cement from the bricks and collecting the cleaned ones. Scorching heat of the sun *assembles the sweating drops on her forehead. She cleans sweat drops with her sari's pallu. Some rolling drops touch her lips; she sucks them with her lips. She turns and, picking up a small pot, drinks some water; quenches her thirst, but is unable to suppress her hunger.' I stopped.*

'You cleverly turned the table on me,' he rebuked.

'Hemu, you're sometimes beyond my understanding?' I grudged.

>*But he was a neat handler of situation.*

'Will you, please, explain the term "destiny"?' he reverted.

'It's kind of a guiding force; call it god, destiny, or fate,' I added.

'You mean, it's like a mystic?'

'No, destiny is not a mystic entity. It's a separate one from all'

'Why does it work upon a human being?'

'Because, man is a mortal entity.'

'Now I got the point,' he said.

'Hemu, you don't appear normal today?'

'Normalcy is a later stage of war.'

'War?'

'Yes, war. Don't you think, life is a dangerous war?'

'How can it be a dangerous one?'

'More hazardous; more dangerous, I say,' he stressed on.

'But, it depends upon man; either to make it hazardous or harmless,' I proposed.

'Sometimes, a man is not responsible for making his life so.'

'No, man is himself responsible, I think!' I cleared.

'Then, you're a lucky person.'

'I hate this word,' I reprimanded.

'But, I like,' he emphasised.

I doubted for a moment that he was right.

The only son to his parents, he was the owner of eighty acres of land.

He was the king who had wealth and prosperity at his disposal.

His marriage with Ketki had grown two years old. And his mother had died of a secret reason last year. Being very sensitive and somewhat shy minded, he had no attachment to his close relatives and had no friends, except me. Ketki, a daughter of a poor parents, entered his life as his life partner, and brought unhappiness and uproar, disturbances, and doubts. Only once, he had spoken about his disturbed married life. Highly proud, bellicose, hot-tempered, suspicious, and distrustful, Ketki defiled his smooth and happy life with her dogged behaviour. Hemant, a poet by nature, was thrown into the cavern of pangs and pathos.

Suddenly, quite from the northern end of the farm, where a long row of teak-wood trees was zooming, a loud drumming sound resonated and Suresh, hurriedly, ran towards that direction. Hemant showed strong reprobation and expressed ruthlessness for the act of men, who were working secretly to shift runlets from the runnel flowing down parallel to the *row of teak-wood trees. Suresh came back and talked about the men who were running riot all the day. It had been an unstopping disturbance for the sincere ryot like Hemant.*

'See, this is the other side of a life' Hemant expressed his truth against those unknown people.

'It's a result of poverty,' I commented.

'This sort of people take poverty as a scam, really!'

'Poverty is my estate; poverty is my blood vein!' I sensed a pride in saying so.

'Don't take my words seriously,' he said normally.

'Hemu, you're the lord of land, but you know better what poverty is!'

'But, poverty- stricken people live more happy life comparatively,' he adduced.

'What happened to you today, saying so sad words?'

He paused, apparently lost in thoughts.

A handsome youth, Hemant might have been grimly shadowed by dark clouds of sorrowful twinges.

His nonchalant manner thrust many doubts into my mind.

A very few reasons known to me were doubted in my mind vagrantly, but how could I dare to ask him.

'Ajju, will you, please, sing a song of your choice for me?' he asked me.

'Hemu, you know better my exam is just a week ahead. I must go now?' I said.

'Oh, sorry, for this trouble,' he apologised.

'But, tell me clearly, what's that troubling you?' I asked.

He had a sad look at the lush-green farm.

*A gentle gust of wind sprang upon the cotton
plants and the rustle sounded sonorously.
I tried to box up my doubts. Because it
was too dark for me to read his face!*

'Anything wrong going on in home?' I dared ask him.

'You know better about my family life!' he said.

'But, this is life, Hemu. You've to carry it on!'

'How?'

'Anyhow!'

'I'm fed up of all these daily quarrels.'

'Such quarrels are needy comings of married life!'

'But, I feel I'm a caged bird—a bird married to a wrong match.'

'It's said that marriages are made in the heaven and performed upon the earth!'

'If it is so, I'm not a man of earth?'

'What's exactly troubling you?' I finalised my inquiry.

His voice was far, far too sad.

I was tired, but I pretended to be more energetic letting my eyes gay, pushing back with a zestful gesture my black oily hair. Even in that sad moment, I saw a flock of chirping birds perched on the branches of a mango tree. The birds' high-sounding chirping was whistling a new meaning of life; a far jolly life than a man's life. How a free and heavenly life the birds live! A life far away from hate, malice, pride, cruelty, wrath!

Suresh brought a tray of fruits.

Hemant, with the fixed look of sad thought, continued, 'Why do I always stress on happiness?'

'Because happiness is man's right!' I said.

'Let me be taken to that market where happiness is
being sold,' he added in a tone of one bitterly hurt.
'I'm afraid, it mustn't be sold out!'

He, then, looked up to the sky and was lost
in grave reflection like an abject person.

What I knew was nothing.

I turned in some surprise and did not
answer clearly for an instant or two.

Recognising his mood, I jibbed
at saying anything more.

He took, one beautiful leather pocket, out of
his shirt's pocket, and held before his eyes.

'See, my mother's face? How beautiful was my mother?'
showing me a photograph, he murmured in pain.

'Who can avoid death?' I consoled him.

'But she died of unknown reason.'

'How can you say so?'

'Doctor had told me that she was alright, when she was
last visited the doctor.'

'Doctor is not a god!'

'But, death doesn't come without reason.'

'Reason alone is not itself a finality of death!'

'My wife has become my enemy, at last. She has troubled
my mother more—more—more—'

His deep voice grew more raucous.
Instinctively, tears gathered in his eyes.
His heart might have been bled with pain?
How bluntly he disclosed the fact that his
wife, Ketki, had troubled his mother?

*How difficult it was for me to control
him in that sensible condition!
Dumbfounded, I looked at his
beautifully built farmhouse.*

*Silence reigned over for a few minutes.
Over then, a shrill screech sounded as the car
stopped suddenly at the door of the farmhouse.
Ketki came out of the car accompanied by
one strong and stout young fellow.*

'Oh, you're here! How are you, my dear?' coming close to Hemant, Ketki roared in a harsh tone. And, then, turning to me, she smiled attackingly. 'Oh, you too?' yelled she like a fishwife.

*That strong and stout young man, who accompanied
her, gave a contemptuous look at me deliberately.*

Hemant rose up.

'Will you, please, have a large or small peg?' Ketki unabashedly pelted her words.

'I'm sorry, Hemant. I must walk my way home!' I said.

'Oye, smart bootlicker! You're the only trouble-shooter, aren't you?' Ketki abhorred me. 'You made my husband so careless. You transformed my uxorious husband into monomaniac; a slave to that worst kind of writing; your so-called scholarship made him too rustic to whisk his wife from a real life.'

Hemant ran to my rescue.

'I brought him in here. Why do you blame him? I trust he is a sober boy.'

'O, sober boy! But wot he has to do here?' Ketki roared.

How termagant she was!

It was an acerbic attack on me. I left the farm quickly.
Ketki presented herself like a virago!

FRIEND IS A MEMBER OF FAMILY.
FRIEND IS A RESCUER, NOT A KILLER.
FRIEND IS A SUPPORTER, NOT AN ENEMY.
FRIEND IS A CONFIDANTE, NOT A RIVAL.

My struggle of waiting went on.
The whole bus station was then turned
up into the big crowded market.
A GREAT PLACE OF ENTERTAINMENT
The sky was growing dark again, sinking
lower and lower over the earth.
Too dark was it for me to see my future.
I strolled back and stood by the corner-
poster of a pan-parlour.

Four men, carrying their big and heavy bags, thick
files, small tiffin containers, came hurriedly and sat on
the floor without caring for dirt and dust, just before
me. They were office clerks. One of them was heavily
drunk. The strong dose of *desi daru* overruled him.
His mouth was full of *pan*. He was making his mouth
acrobatic to spit on. Other one was a skinny man, who
was chewing *kharra*. Looking around, he carelessly
cleared sputum from his throat and smiled at me,
shrugging his shoulders heroically. The very next to
him was a dark-skinned, bellied man, who was smoking
a costly cigarette. He looked quite arrogant. His red

eyes and dark face made him ugly. And the fourth one was a tall but a slim man. His shrunken face, thick lips, leaned body, and worried look made him simply a puppeteer. All were passengers, who were travelling up and down to their offices from their native places. All of them seemed quite worried and careworn and unhappy.

They opened their talk.

'See, what's our luck! We've to be on duty even on the day like *Ghatsthapana*,' *Desi Daruwala* opened a dialogue, 'My leaves are limited. All are wasted in travel and travel—busy work. Tomorrow, my daughter's admission is on? I need one lakh and fifty thousand for that. Higher education of any sort does not remain for a common man—a man like me?'

'Lakh, fifty thousand,' stressing hard on the words, *Kharrawala* joined, 'are nothing more—nothing more! Five to ten lakh are being paid by the people today only for a simple admission and tuition classes to eleventh and twelfth. Engineering and medical faculties are no more for us, no more? All are dreams for us! Only admissions to government colleges can do help for us. But, our *pottey saaley*! What can be said *bhou*—what can be said—all can't reach to that level. That's also a rat race. All is beyond our reach! Can't even imagine purchasing an admission form? And simply, my daughters are not so much studious. They're dull. They waste much of their time in watching TV programmes and *bakwas* serials!'

He sneezed hard.

Cigarettewala, stylishly threw a burning
bit of a cigarette away carelessly.
And *Kharrawala* hurried to the
corner to spit a sputum.

'Medical colleges, engineering colleges are beyond our reach really!' *Cigarettewala* opened his words, 'Wherefrom we sum the money for such a costly education? *Yer* right *bhou*! Truly, *or* children aren't so talented and hard-working. All mediocre! I'd some aspirations of my own. My *gharwali* also wanted the same as I wanted! But only aspirations don't work. Children should understand how they've to travel on right road? They should choose their own way. What else can we do, but advising merely? Only money can't do all; it needs hard work and desired ambition. Otherwise, spending money is a *riks*!'

A kind of a snobbish gait empowered
the *Puppeteer's* body.
Desi-daruwala staggered up on the ground.

'I'm really very lucky in that sense!' the *puppeteer* proudly continued his spell, 'My children have acquired what they wanted. Elder son is mechanical engineer and the younger is software engineer, working in reputed companies and both are getting good pocket (*package*). I've no daughter. No *riks* of hasting marriage. No burden. Only two sons—*kamate hai; kissa khattam.*'

'*Teri baat aur hai ya-arr—teri baaat aur hai! Lekin*— what can we people do—when our *pottey* gone mad and rubbish? My elder son, *ye* know all, has no work at all. He's only *twelve* pass. For his settlement, I took loan from Alahabad Bank and purchased a matador for him—looking forward to bring him on the right track? See, that idle boy couldn't get the business—didn't work hard. Instead, he burdened me with some more loans of other banks. Squandered money on *sattta, lottery* and what not—tell *ye,* frankly. Actually, this is not a public talk? But what a helpless father can talk? Joined bad company and wasted time, squandered money—*bhou*—exploited me? Sold out matador and now he's just passing time playing *taash* and what not? Only hope is my daughter!' *Desi Daruwala* sadly narrated a spell of his son's story.

    Kharrawala appeared to be a bystander.

      Cigarettewala, a canny and cunning serviceman, might have calculated some strange thoughts in his mind.

    Puppeteer breathed a sense of pride.

'In this competition, we can't survive, really?' the *Cigarettewala* dejectedly opined.

'And I've five daughters—all unmarried. Since last four years, I'm trying for elder daughter's marriage, but couldn't get to manage.' *Kharrawala* extended his worry: 'I spared no efforts to cross the thresholds of even the commonest relatives, but nobody helped. Reversely, all took my test. All demanded money. Wherefrom shall an ordinary clerk like me bring money for spending on dowry? A boy who works simply as a *shikshan sevak* in an ordinary school demands fifty thousand rupees or ornament of worth the same. Dowry money goes high

up to lakh and above. How to shake off this burden—
that's my problem.'

'My elder son exploited me a lot,' panged *Cigarettewala*,
'imagining me a fool! He wanted to take admission for
CA course and that too in Ahmedabad's college. He
tried then spending two *lakh* rupees. But couldn't get the
admission falling short of percentage. He repeated and
again spent money a lot, but the same thing happened.
The second one is also mediocre, failed in B Com first
year twice and now joined arts faculty from this year.
The third one is handicapped. He is in twelfth this year,
ye all know! My three sons are three directions. I have
no hope from them. I'm completely grieved for their
career!'

'Kadam, *yer* somewhat good in position,' advising
to *Cigarettewala*, the *Puppeteer* continued, 'as *ye've*
fifteen acres of land and that too near the city. Good
money *ye* can get selling it. *Ye* know *yer* sons can't
achieve in this education field and get the jobs *ye*
understand, so why don't *yer* try them in business?
Don't mind what *am* suggesting?'

'Raut, that is my only property. What will be my earning
source after my retirement? Only two years more for
retirement *bhau*?' Kadam cleared his point.

'But, Kadam *dada*, at least *yer* sons are trying in
education field. Now education wants money. Let them
try and settle their jobs. They're not like my squandering
son!' said *Desi Daruwallah*.

'Kadam *Seth*, *yer* lucky that *ye've* no daughters—very
lucky! There is no difference between a destitute and

a father of daughters. See my condition?' *Kharrawala* exclaimed mimicking like Asrani.

'Sontakke *bhau*, tell *ye* really: daughters are daughters! No comparison with sons,' Kadam said.

'Right, *yer* Kadam—*yer* right! But one is afraid of the present happenings! Why are the girls committing suicides for simple reasons? Daily there are news in the newspapers that stir *ourr* hearts? My daughter is good in study, but I fear for her future life,' *Desi Daruwala* said, becoming sensitive.

'Nagdive *bhau*, *yer* right! Present time is very difficult to manage everything,' Raut forwarded his opinion.

Kadam leaned against the side of the pillar.

Raut made himself busy in searching out some paper in his canvas bag.

Nagdive, putting his hand wearily on the back of his black heavy bag, rested.

Sontakke rose up and walked around the bus station. After a search for a paper, Raut continued, 'See my elder son sent me a cheque.'

'Worth how much?' Kadam asked anxiously.

'Twenty thousand rupees.'

'So caring *yer* son is!' Nagdive quelled his feeling.

'That's why son is must,' reacted Sontakke.

'But my money goes on medicine purchasing, *yer* know?' Raut said.

'And my wife needs five thousand and more for medicine per month—won't believe?' Kadam said.

'But, I've gone through really very bad economic situations nowadays. Loans from various banks supported me for my sons' education—true. But, every time, I was burdened with a great amount of loan money. Sometimes, I couldn't manage even a sum to repay the instalments of the banks. It was really very hard time for me. Tension, tension, and tension, but god's worship backed me for the repayment of the instalments, I believe! Now the only tension over my head is that I'm suffering from severe diabetes and high blood pressure and just before fortnight the doctor advised me to go for heart bypass surgery urgently. Hush!' Raut cited his worry.

'Tension is the only reason for all this ailments and diseases?' Kadam reacted.

'Today, I feel—I remember my wife,' Raut staggered in voice.

'That depends upon heaven! Right from Nagpur to Bombay, Pune, I took my wife to the famous expert doctors but nothing I got in return. Disease grew more *n* more severe! No control. Cure is far away.' Kadam expressed his sorrow.

'That's why I follow: *drink and be merry*!' Nagdive smiled secretly.

'Little quantity is okay,' Sontakke interpreted, 'but, *yer* a heavy drinker!'

'Control *yer* drinking, Nagdive. Save something for daughter!' Raut advised.

I could hear their words very well.

GLASS FLASHING REALITY

A weariness of their minds would answer
the fitted all conditions of present time!

Miserable variations they were
describing on proletariat status.
PREGNABLE POOR SOULS
LEAVING LIFE LIKE A CAT ON HOT BRICKS

'How can one live, bear, all troubles, cutting short the doses? *Dessi* is my breath; my life.' Nagdive babbled.

'*Ye* see, life piles on life. This heavy drinking problem will lead another problem. Then? *Yer* will lick the dust of my condition. It's all very costly and torturous—this surgery *n* all! It's a curse?' Raut advised him.

'My mother is 81. Still she is living but takes no medicine *n* my wife—don't ask. Swallows medicine *n* medicine—today this and tomorrow that—don't ask? Only tension *n* tension!' Sontakke reacted.

'Tension-free life is impossible! My sons never take care of even their mother. She is suffering from acute psoriasis and lives under tension,' Kadam continued his pangs, 'and has recently a severe attack. I'm very much under tension nowadays and over this unseasonable rain, crops are destroyed—that's other tension made me mad, *bhou*!'

'We've no facility of loaning money from other banks,' Nagdive stressed his urgent need, 'and now when only two years remained for retirement—dare not take a loan from my bank. And only nine thousand aren't sufficient to bear expenditure—all salary goes in the deduction of loan instalments. My daughter is studious and wants to be an engineer. Maximum two lakhs are urgently needed for her admission—but?'

'This children's education growing on a great tension,' Raut, cursing his destiny, said, 'and placed a never ending situation of repaying the loan amount before us. My case is very dominant for such loaning! On the one hand, there is satisfaction that my sons are employed; on the other, there is only repentance and test of forbearance—how a wifeless man living his life's final phase of life under the burden n heavy tension? Else isn't good—nothing good.'

All were expressing their grief persuasively.

COGENT WORDS

Outside opposite to the pan-parlour, there
rose a quarrel between two young boys.
The usual case of pick-pocketing!
The sound and the fury!
Raut projected himself like an altruist.
Kadam appeared to be an ambivert.
Sontakke personalised himself as misanthrope.
Nagdive presented himself as introvert.

'Look at this father of five daughters! And just imagine,' clearing his throat, Sontakke continued, 'how this *poor soul* manages all the burdens? Raut *dada* knows about my second daughter's case how under depression she attempted to commit suicide. Fifty thousand rupees spent on her treatment, still the burning marks remained unclear—that blackened her face. Luckily, she could escape death. And my loudmouth wife had held me responsible for her depression and the happening, saying I couldn't try for her marriage! All my expenditure runs on only my salary—having no other earning source.

The first daughter has become overaged. Sometimes I feel this marriage system is all fake—false—fad—should be denounced?'

Sontakke, a senior clerk working in
Panchayat Samiti, narrated his story.

'See, my condition isn't different than *yers*. My 30-year-old son,' Kadam spoke, 'squanders money like anything. And Nagdive *bhau*, *ye* helped him last year, when he was caught red handed in a theft's case. It was my luck—that the police inspector, who released him, had been found to be Nagdive *bhau*'s cousin brother. My wife couldn't bear a shock. Her diabetes became more severe and her sugar reached to 450 and above. A complete month had been wasted in her treatment. The younger one had posed another problem that he was beaten by one cloth merchant severely for molesting his daughter. I suffered a great insult. See, therefore, I say daughters are better than sons—see. My wife won't breathe more air—she will—'

Kadam, a head clerk in HSSC Board,
normally expressed his sorrow.

'More or less the same is my son's case. I've already talked about his squandering of money. But the saddest thing is his relationship with that widow—' Nagdive reacted, 'named Geeta. He is under her love. I tried and tried to pull him back from that relationship—but, no—instead, he turned to be a traitor. I haven't dirty habit of washing dirty linen in public, but—as *yer* all my friends—it's not bad to tell *ye* that he had beaten me last week for refusing to give him fifty

thousand rupees—see—this is the only son—see—
and my wife—never speak on anything—no support—
unsupportive soul—me a man in hell!'

Nagdive, a senior clerk in cooperative bank,
    introspectively cited his son's traits.

'Every life is discovered to be under hard cares,
anxieties, sorrows. No soul under the sun breathes a
worriless life. And how many of us know the secret of
true happiness? I always went along stretching my hand
to helping others. I seldom looked for my own interests.
Worked harder for my sons and my work brought to me
a sweet fruit—but, see my dear brothers—what an ugly
revenge time has taken against me—my wife didn't
die a natural death—she committed *suicide* because of
acute pain caused by breast cancer—see!'

Raut, a head clerk in one grant-in-aid private college,
    altruistically disclosed the secret of his wife's death.

The talk of those four took me minutes to
    get over it—simply heart-throbbing!
It was my fault, wholly and solely my fault,
    that I had been away from home.
I must be absolutely candid with
    home situation, I thought.
I walked slowly down to the parking lane.
    Most horrible picture of home was
    piercing my eyeballs—horrible!
A splash of rainwater sprinkled on
    my face. I shivered. I feared.

With care I pressed my tiny file close to my chest
and moved back to the crowded benches.
Triumph of seating choice was befooling me.
I stood beside a bench resting my right hand on it.
But just as when I turned to my right, a young
boy abused me in a derogatory term.

'Can't you see I'm busy in my talking to?' the boy
hooted.

'But, this is not a manner of speaking to others?' I
revolted.

'One minute, I tell you what is manner,' he reacted.

I stood quietly.

He began to speak on his smartphone.

*Hi—ur the most beautiful girl ever seen—just you—just
you—ur a stunner—dream girl—my sweet heart—my
darling—my dream queen—I'm busy—yaar—very
busy—just now I'm in college—just attended math
period—what—I'm very good kilometres away from
you—be so long—how can I—no darling—no—no—
believe me—don't take me as cheater—I don't know
anything about her—no—no—never met—believe me—
what—what do u say—I'm a snorer—ha—ha—ha—a
psychopath—lootera—scavenger—say—dear—say—
whatever u want—say—murderer—now—darling—
this is—too much—yeh—yeh—now—u came on line—
that's right—that's right—superman—yeh—rightly—
I'm a superman—ha—ha—snaking out for a drink—no
ma'am—no—no desi—no foreign—what—u—want—
die—what—jumping off the balcony—labaad—
many want it—what's new—monotonous—daily*

routine—thirty five thousand spent on this new smartphone—u know—how much do you know—old was sold—hopeless—market—way in the market— new—fine—apps are—in the market—many dating apps—dating app—must darling—must—dating app is must—for a smart boy like me—and a girl like u—urgent need—chhodo yaar—who cares for society—public— relatives—father—never know—how can she—easy to befool mother—easily—why should I tell u—secret— secret means secret—what—arrey yaar—believe me— oh yeas—becoz—I'm superman—love u yaar—deeply love u—can't fathom—king—king of love—ha—ha— ha—yeh, that's right—love u—love u—ok—ok—new number—ok—but—tomorrow—by word—without fail—saali—cheat—sairrat yaar—really—sairrat—

He ceased his talk on his smartphone.

As soon as he pressed a close button of his smartphone, a caller tune rang again. Seeing a number on the screen, he closed the phone and looked around and then he stylishly thrust his hand into his jersey's pocket to get himself a cigarette and without caring about anyone who seated on the bench and the public around, he lighted a cigarette. He glanced at the crowd as if he were an emperor of that surrounding region. Careless, obtrusive manner—sad—sad! Even the tone of his speaking was quite robust.

I partly altered my standing position.
I became haggard and restless and
my eyes had the troubled look.

HOW THE BUSINESS OF LOVE IS EXPLODING
RIGHTLY A SEISMIC EXPLOSION
DATING APPS: NEW CUPIDS

How the young generation started playing with the play-stores on their mobile phones—all time busy bursting with dating and dating? (The parents, busied with the problem of keeping body and soul together, have no slightest idea of what apps are. What they call it 'judging people on apps) Recently, I had read in the magazine : question : what sort of a man are you looking for? Answer: anyone who puts up a photograph shirtless, naked, or half-naked even or with six-pack abs is out. And the boys adjectively call it 'simply pleasant!' Apps are being used to send sexual messages and comments on women's bodily attributes. *(Tinder, Trulymadly, Woo are being used by millions of youths in the world.)*

A double revolution indeed!

'So, what do you say about my manners?' the boy impugned. He uttered severe derogatory words in his mouth and cast an angry look at me. A middle-heighted, weak boy was behaving like a strong boxer!

I made no answer. I smiled.

How could I descend to the level of that robust soul?

His imminent attack was mitigated by
my behaviour and easy smile.
I formed at that moment much the
same picture as I imagined.
Subduing my anguish, I stood
calm observing the crowd.

At that moment, another boy joined him,
who was carrying one big box with him.

'Searching you *yaar*! I was searching you for the last two hours!' the new boy quelled.

'You bastard, I was waiting outside for a long,' he said, handling his costly smartphone.

'She said she won't come today?'

'Why, why, she won't come today. No meaning for my love!' he reflected a surprise.

'Secret, her brother comes to know about you *maalum hai*?'

'This lying is a disease, *yaar*; no any antibiotic can cure it!' he scratched his head.

'Her brother is very cunning—remember—*bacchana padega tereko usase, bolta mai?*'

'*Bhot dekhe aise tismarkhaan—sabko ludhakata mai, ek din,*' the boy fiercely reverted.

But he looked bewildered and stunned.

Then he tried one number on his smartphone.

bhai—ye—bhai—I'm here—speaking—speaking—sound not audible—yeh—market—durga devi—yeh—right—nine four—sure—right number—call—you—okay—danger—public danger—tomorrow—right bhai—right—see—will see—keeping eyes—won't go—won't go—giving—giving your—call—won't see—won't see—believe—me—done—surely done—subject closed—surely—won't live—surely—

He ceased.

A strange stillness hung over the bus station.

Standing at the massive pillar like an interested
spectator, I observed the boy's action.

With much probing and plucking, that beleaguered
boy managed to speak his words filtrately.

'Tell me, shall I go?' the other boy asked him.

'Won't you support me in this work?' he questioned.

'Risk? A great risk? I can't say?'

'I know, the timid ones always run away even at the
slightest sign of danger.'

'Whatever you think.'

'It needs bold and solid heart, you dull boy.'

'To harm is easier and simpler, but escape from it is
very difficult.'

'This Durga Devi festival days are enough for that
mission.'

'See, I'm not the partner in your mission.'

'Okay, I alone will do that!'

Something most improper and egregious
had been cooking there in his mind!

Doubtlessly when he spoke, he turned the contents
of his talk more secretive and susceptible.

His last sentence appeared to me to be so suspenseful
that I could hardly believe that he was a common boy.

I saw he drew a long breath and wiped
the perspiration from his forehead.

'How often have I said to you that there is clearly a
danger ahead and it's not better to join his gang; you
waived my proposition. Now time is gone out of hand;
do it or get ready for punishment,' his mate warned.

He jerked his arms in a kind of violent frenzy.

There sang a caller tune of his smartphone again.
*Huum—speaking—what happened—urgently—
home—for what—tell me—directly—oh, no—father's
health—serious—why—he was—okay yesterday—
what happened to—that Buddha—old—worst man—
serious—nothing will—happen so soon—that bastard
old man—my father—is hopeless man—won't die soon—
serious—to hospital—who took him—to hospital—faltu
dhanda—won't care—let him die—useless man—yes—
let him die—I'm busy—won't come—no time—wasting
time—father—let him die—father—don't know—said
father—*

He closed his smartphone and stamped
his feet in a sheer feat of anguish.
Suddenly, he broke out into a suppressed querulous
cry and madly ran towards the gate of the bus station.
His words took me completely by surprise.

NEW YEAR DAY
1 JANUARY 2012

*Anna coughed heavily and cleared his throat.
He was working carefully on his efforts to protect the
collected cotton from the drops of rain dripping from
the tainted tiled roof. His care-smitten face was bold
enough to express the glen of tears. I knew his health
was adversely affected by the cares and burdens. I tried
to help him but he said, 'No, don't waste your time in
such work,' and smiled adoringly. His hands rose to
wish me. 'Go, do your work.'*

'Father, how long this will go?' I said imploringly.

'Food is costly; so way is difficult.'

'You always say that it's unwise to blame your luck, because there is no such thing as luck.'

'Dependence on luck makes man lame in action,' he advised.

'And only action makes man helpless?'

'No, that's not right. No action makes man helpless, but it paves the way to leading a life on front.'

'Is there no end for action?'

'No, action is endless.'

'Is there no end for hard work?'

'Action and hard work go hand in hand. They are inseparable.'

'Only hard work and no reward?'

'Reward follows the work and action.'

'But not in time?'

'Patience is a brother to time.'

'What about your hard work?' I asked analytically.

'That's in my hand,' he paused, apparently lost in thought and continued, 'work, work, work, and win over the life. Because I'm a soldier in the battlefield called life. And soldier's duty is to fight on front' he said.

'And who's the General, who paddles a canoe of this battle in the battlefield?'

'Of course, one of the soldiers who fights?'

'No, father, the General is our birth.'

I forwarded my argument.

'No, I don't agree. Birth never says to stop anywhere.'

'What about your hard work?' I repeated the same question.

He looked far away through the dripping roof
and stretched out his hands as if he was praying
to god. Mother hobbled off to the kitchen.

'Babu, your meal is ready,' Maa.

'I think you're already late, today?' Anna.

He looked helpless.

It rained heavily last night.

'Won't go today?' said I.

'Okay, take rest then,' Maa.

'Rain won't allow any work today?' Anna.

I called my father Anna.

He coughed, coughed, and coughed.

After a streak of coughing, he cleared his mouth.

'Anna, you don't take your medicine regularly,' said I complainingly.

'Take a cup of ginger tea, and it will be in control,' Maa.

He sighed. He paused. He mumbled.

'Maya wants to join a job,' mother said.

'I know, but any job has become a great problem,' I began explaining, 'and a job in teaching field demands much money. Now, see my problem? I'm qualified. I'm ready to go anywhere. I need job urgently. But, I'm unemployed. Wandering like a wild animal for the last six years. Maya is also qualified. She also has done some of the courses needed for clerkship and teachership. Agree, but where will she get a job?'

Maya was sure I was well aware
of the present situation.

'Job is alright, but I've to look forward for her marriage first. I really shall have to see her as a wedded girl. Time will not permit a good chance after wasting this favourable one.' Anna.

'I will be a relieved soul if she gets married this summer,' expressing her will, Maa said, *'Daughters are after all the property of other's home. All have to depart from father's home after marriage indeed.'*

'Anna, what happened to that boy who had contacted you last month? He is employed I think?' I enquired.

'No reply from him, yet. But, I found him unsuitable for Maya. He is a liar'

'We have to seek for other suitable boys, then.'

'It's a must.'

'But, don't take pressure.'

'Two years are gone for a search of a suitable boy—no match is found yet—she would tie a wedding knot—see for—this year—it's essential—this year,' Maa spoke in breaks as she had a severe breathing problem.

'A man should not sink into any condition so bad that it could not be rectified. A gloomy foreboding must not be awaited!' Anna carried on, *'She is just par the marriage age, running twenty-eighth winter now!'*

'Yeh, that is so?' Maa.

A tension passed for a moment over all's faces.

'Maya is qualified and good looking and hard-working too—hoping to get it well this summer,' I said.

'Anna, don't let the tension mounting on?' sitting closer to him, Mamta said.

'No, children, don't worry for me. Nothing will happen to me. Maya's marriage definitely be get over this summer. Every father wants his daughter happy. And I'll do my best to find a suitable match to her,' Anna.

Suddenly he stopped talking and
gazed out over the tainted roof.
His eyes felt as if they would burst from straining
so hard into the faint light passing from the roof.

'Last year Shankar Anasane's elder daughter got married to a boy working in a private factory. He gave three lakhs and expenditure of marriage extra,' Maa.

'Dowry money is a need of today. Nobody can stop dowry system whatever are the cries of the people. It's a matter to be accepted. We will also have to adjust money, at least, three lakhs before this summer,' Anna.

'And how can you?'

'It needed to be anyhow?'

'We've a little gold?' Maa.

'No, your gold will not be sold out,' Anna.

'Then, what's the other way?'

'Ways are many: but which one be adopted, that's the problem?'

The great ordeal was in front of us!
Anna glanced swiftly again over the roof, running
his eyes up and down the sheaves of cotton.
I felt it unlikely that he did so.
Maa put down her work of winnowing rice
and rolled on her eyes round the dinette.
Maya and Mamta were busy in helping mother.

It is, of course, socially very acceptable problem of curbing dowry system. Moreover it had become a fundamental rule of life and people approached the way. All knew about their bad approach and resulted in bad response. How to deal with this system became a problem. Marriageable young girls fell a prey to it.

3.00 p.m.

Rain abated.

'Let me go to the field, my works remained incomplete?' Anna.

'No, don't go today. It's still raining.' Maa.

'This is a slow shower. I must go.'

'No, Anna. Tell me I will have done your work completed,' I said.

'Anna, you take complete rest today. You're not well,' Maya suggested.

'Babu, see, his medicine has to be purchased by two days.' Maa.

'Sure, tomorrow I will bring.'

'Don't waste your money on medicine? I'm okay!'

'Anna, doctor advised you to complete a dose.'

'It's urgent, Dada. Bring medicine tomorrow,' Maya.

Anna had an attack of coughing again.

And then of a sudden, a group of boys appeared at the door.

'Oh, Dada, you're at home today!' Sameer, my old classmate, exclaimed.

'Today, we've arranged a New Year Party at Gram Panchayat Bhavan,' said Kunal, the son of Sarpanch.

*'We are collecting contribution for party. Only hundred
rupees you have to contribute,' Yeshwant said.*

*'At eight, in the Panchayat Bhavan Hall, the party will
start,' Vijay, my junior in the middle school, said.*

All other boys were dancing their steps in merriment.

*It happened so suddenly that I couldn't
give way even to speak a word.*

*'See, Sameer, I'm busy in my work today. I'm sorry I
can't join your party!' I said.*

*'It's New Year Party, yaar! Come on!' Vijay exhibited
his enthusiasm.*

'But, I've problem.'

*'All this is new, believe! Our New Year Party will go to
a new sensation,' Yeshwant danced a step.*

*'See, a lot has happened to this village a few months
ago. Don't forget those grievous moments!' I said.*

*My words didn't work upon them.
Instead, they all started dancing.*

*'Sad happenings are to be forgotten. Rejoice a rising
day, that's enough!' Sameer said and looked at me.*

'Only hundred rupees you've to pay,' Yeshwant.

*'It's not the question of hundred rupees, but I feel guilty
to celebrate a moment under a sad background. Hardly
a month ago, our village has seen a suicidal death of
our dear, Eknath?' I said forcefully.*

*Saying, 'We are at the wrong door,'
they all disappeared.*

*It was, indeed, high time that someone
like me incapable of giving advice.*

Yet upon that afternoon, I felt that
something would happen suddenly.
The weather was too cold to be
malodorous and malicious.
Anna rose up and looked at the dripping drops of
rain water with his weak eyes, muttering some words
under his tongue. He took a sheaf of cotton in his hand
and uttered, 'How far will this white gold support my
children—my family?' and suddenly, he fell down on the
ground writhing in severe pain. Pressing hard on his
chest, he groaned, groaned, and groaned. Maa cried
heavily, 'Babu, come, see what happened?'
'O, my god! This is terrible!' I cried.
Late in the night, we admitted Anna
to the government hospital.
He had suffered a severe myocardial infarction fit.

FATHER, THOU ART A SOUL TOUGHER,
SANG AND TAUGHT ME A GREAT LESSON.
HOW TO FORGE AHEAD SWIFTER
WITH COGENT AND STRONG RESOLUTION.

Rain's notorious dance strengthened its rhythm again.
I just walked to the enquiry window.

I saw a big poster of the advertisement of
insecticide which was hung on the uneven wall of
the inquiry window of the bus station. One reputed
company's pompous advertorial big posters of
insecticides and fertilisers were beautifying that
wall spot. The poisonous protection for crops. These

insecticides of different kinds have become a big question for farmers, a big dilemma for users. The common farmers can't use very expensive insecticides and fertilisers and thus can't yield good production protecting the crops. Only rich and middle class farmers can afford the prices of insecticides and can opt for different companies. The crops like cotton, wheat, soybean, hybrid, and other vegetable crops need costly insecticides for more protection and more production. The insecticides and fertilisers are at the pivot of the present agriculture system. No crop is protected without using terribly poisonous insecticides and fertilisers. Organic fertilisers are being replaced by such harmful fertilisers. More crops, more production, more profit, more money has become an agricultural dictum. The common farmers have no idea of what way they are using these terrible insecticides. Unknowingly, all are running after the venomous red triangle insecticides. Is it merely a business or really in a true sense a progress of farming?

Having read scrupulously the advertisement of insecticide, I tried to hunt the reasons behind the unceasing series of farmers' suicides. The colourful printed advertorial pamphlets, posters, and covered bottles of insecticides and finely printed sacks of fertilisers attracted the farmers and looking safe production into those sacks and bottles, all looked forward to enrich the dreams of a productive future. And for this, they ran to the various banks for loans and stepped in the thresholds of cunning *sawakars*.

The burden of loans and meagre production corrupt their minds and bodies and pulled them into the valley of death. Some poor and wretched faces of farmers, who committed suicide in my small village, manifested before my eyes. Last year, Shankar committed suicide by drinking poisonous insecticide, leaving three marriageable daughters and an unemployed son behind at their own risk as his wife had already met death for a severe heart attack. The young Vikas committed suicide by throwing himself onto the railway track, making his parents tear down their whole life. The big burden of the loan from various banks made Ballu Patil's way to death by drowning into the well. Ballu was a true hard-working farmer as well as a faithful man. And Ajabrao Tale accepted death by hanging for a regular tension of his wife's illness. Under the constant burden of loans and family problems, all poverty-stricken farmers made their way to surrender to death, the final exit from life.

All danced in my eyes and soon they disappeared.

poverty—poverty—poverty—took—our—lives—cried—money—money—money—all cried—

Their cries hummed into the air.

Standing again at the pillar, I gazed at the moving crowd. The harsh rustle of engines, bumper sounding horns of the buses, the high-sounding yell of the vendors, the bucolic bustling of passengers, turned the place into the biggest spot for any kind of entertainment.

Those were four in number, the farmers, who sat
on the dirty floor, just a few feet away from me.
Their wrinkled faces and sunken eyes, tattered clothes,
and sun-burnt tense bodies were enough to narrate their
pangs and pathos—the unsung heroes of the farming
battlefield. One could easily mark a glaring hope on
their faces for downing showers of unseasonal rain.
Those tense and tired faces made me irresistible to
know their worsened hopes—words—words—words.

FOUR FARMERS

'Sonba Anna, how many bags of *soyabean* have you
sowed in your three acres of land?' the first questioned
with a doubt roaring in his head for wasting costly
seeds.

'No use of asking, Mahadev—no use, now? Purchased
good-quality seed this time and sowed in time, but June
went rainless; July had acutely scanty rain; August
had only two showers of rain; and September went
completely dry; rain deceived us fully. The second
sowing rode on my chest, don't ask.' Sonba's voice
quavered, 'Money spent on seeds washed away—
washed away. Wherefrom shall a man adjust the
purchasing of seed for the second time? The seed is so
expensive, so costly, and I had no money for purchasing
it for the second round. Right time sowing is a golden
way in farming, but rain snatched everything away
from us, transforming everything into the waste.'

'Mahadev Dada, do you expect anything further when this season went dry and dirty left nothing better for us?' the third quivered sadly, 'and who can save us from penury?'

'Ganpat, such mood of season can't be avoided. That's a rock-solid status for us! Neither you or me nor anybody can try even to vanish this curse upon us, you know?' the fourth moaned and compressed a pinch of tobacco into his lower lip. 'See, interest rates of *sawakars* are touching the sky. What can we do anymore but to lend money and kick out the expenditure of daily doings and severe struggle for life?'

'See, see outside, how forcefully it's triggering now on this odd day!' Sonba lampooned on fierce attack of rain, 'And on the time of farming season *ssalla!* All disappeared and rode upon our chests! Irregularity and scanty rain make us mad! It's all the story of rain all the years and crops are being corrupt regularly. Dogs' life the farmers are destined to live and always they shed tears for the unwanted deaths—curse!'

'No season showers any good blessings anymore on farmers, really it's curse!' Mahadev continued his wounded words, 'Everything is right for others. All get rewards on time, but these *badnaseeb* farmers have no other benefit and no specific facility that will help them, nothing—bare—bare from all sides—thus—accepting deaths—all dying—all the days—meekly—numb mind—dumb life.'

'Right Mahadev, your every word is right. Farmers' condition is worsening day by day,' Sonba clearing his coughing throat said, 'No money, no help, no support, and this inflation? On rise and no fall? No value of rupee? Scanty rain and rising loans from various banks will surely pierce our hearts and one day will take us to the graveyard. What can I earn from only *soyabean* production and that too merely from five acres of cultivation—three acres for *soyabean* and two acres for *cotton*?'

'Ganpat, what will happen to us?' Mahadev asked.

'Can't foretell?' Ganpat replied.

'We must try to make our lives safer?' Sonba articulated in a politician's tone.

'Right you're, Sonba Anna, right you're!' Ganpat stuttered in a very conjoint tone.

'Last year, heavy hailstorm accompanied by rain and high-speed winds unleashed the crops and devastated the farmers' hopes. Even Nature takes revenge upon us.'

<blockquote>
Clearing his running nose,
Ganpat looked at the mizzle.
And then squirmed a little on the place.
Others sighed desperately.
</blockquote>

'God's curse falls upon us!' Sonba again spoke in an utter agony.

'Nobody comes to our risk at the sight of any danger?' Keshav broke his long silence.

'We became the puppet in the hands of fortune. This came to our fate—rise in the morning—work in the field for a day in and day out—long, long—and take an interrupted sleep under the regular burden of unceasing liabilities, burdens, and problems, work, work, and work; and no rest, even an animal has a rest,' Mahadeo cried in painful words.

'And how can we earn only to keep body and soul together?' Keshav questioned.

'*Money set the root of all evil,*' Sonba cited a maxim.

'*A drowning man catches at a straw*—all right, but what means of escape left for a farmer to cope with extremely difficult situations presented by natural calamity like this?' Keshav said in revulsion.

'Ours is a land of mainly cotton production, but can't do anything for want of monetary support, Ganpat? Lots of money needed right from sowing to the harvest season, and much labour be then put in, isn't it? And see the money, the farmers are wasting on mere charges of workmen and the labourers. Wages are reaching up the sky?' The anxiety-stricken face of Keshav revealed all pangs of the worsened monetary condition of farmers.

'And how much can we lend from the banks? And how much can be repaid?' Ganpat said.

'Problem?' Sonba coughed and coughed and carelessly spit on the floor pressing his chest hard.

'Difficult! Really, it's become difficult to save the life from mere cultivation of land?' reacted Mahadev.

'Where shall a sane farmer go this season?' Ganpat said.

'Saving life from all these odds has become a problem.' Sonba said and coughed again.

Keshav took out a *whiff* of his shirt's pocket and lighted and dragged a heavy puff into the chest.

'Mahadeo,' yelped Keshav, 'How much have you spent on your treatment so far? And still not any recovery—reveals your body.'

'Don't ask,' said Mahadeo with a little lisp, 'No recovery, even after spending fifty thousand rupees (*clearing his voice*). All time busy in dashing the doors of doctors. General hospital is not at all useful for any patient, I tell you. Run to the private hospital and get recovered. It's the only way for recovery, but the private hospitals are so costly that we common people can't bear expenses, still no guarantee of recovery.'

Mahadeo couldn't control his tears.
Rolling tears on his sun-burnt cheeks
stunned the other three.
And their faces shrunk with unknown fears.
All looked worrisome and careworn.

'This is a real problem. Doctors in private hospitals don't care for poor people. They want only *paisewalah*—isn't it? And what else we know about the diseases and ailments? What we know about medicines? And what we know about medical markets? Prices and bills and dummy medicines. All loot!' cried Sonba.

'And this year, I don't think rain will support us. See the beginning of October taking revenge against us. This is just the start of unseasonable rain. What's the guarantee of rain? *Soyabean* decayed and washed out. Cotton need not to be wasted. I've only four acres of land and my complete family is relying on the production and no other support. Little money support—what do I do? Loan is mounting on head. Fifty thousand rupees raised on my head. Now no sparing door I left to knock for further lending. Where shall I go for relief? No escape. No way to avoid all. What remains then? End of— *sshh*?' summarised Keshav, his agonised condition and hid his face into his cotton *shela*.

'Just yesterday, that happened, very terrible indeed!'

'Just terrible!'

'Suicide! One more went on the same line.'

'Shivram finished his role early.'

'Hardly, he was forty-five?'

'It's not the matter of age? It's the matter of tolerance and perseverance, you know?'

'But, he was tired of his family; what can be said?'

'His wife made him mad actually. What can a man do when god hasn't gifted a son to him? And what one has to do with a son? Already he has six daughters. And what happened now? What about those six daughters left behind?' Mahadeo.

'Man accepts death when he sees no other way to escape from situations—and ends life this way,' Sonba.

'A farmer's death has become the international news today!' Keshav.

'And difficult problem, too!' Tukaram.

'See, death is death. But, we have made it worldwide. It's clear that nobody comes to your help after death. We can cite many examples,' Sonba pelted a remark.

'All consider us as foolish? Never try to see at the cause? Speeches and slogans are not enough to curb this problem. Is it enough to bark only comments and slogans on deaths?' Mahadeo.

'We ourselves have to seek for remedies?' Keshav.

'Right, Keshav Dada, you're right!' Tukaram.

'And the only remedy on this problem is to get a good price for our crops, I say,' Sonba.

'Sonba, do you expect this?' Keshav.

'It's mere expectation.'

'Just look at the market. Systematically cotton's price will be pulled down at the peak hours.'

'Same will happen to *soyabean*, *moong*, *channa*, *tuwar,flaxseed*—same thing—whatever.'

'And this unseasonable rain.'

'Weather and world—both are adversaries to farmers.'

'That's the root cause of our death?'

'But don't you think, Tukaram, we are wasting our lives for the trivial matters?' Sonba.

'Right! Reasons are already there but our way of treatment to them is wrong, I suppose!' Tukaram.

'Cotton is highly paid but needs costly cultivation—unprofitable at last?' Keshav.

'It depends upon good and right time rainfall and solid cultivation,' Mahadeo.

'See, what comes this year to our share?' Sonba.

'We ourselves must run for quick remedies for diverting a decline.'

'Yeh, we must try to reinvent the ways to cultivation with a hope.'

'Whatever it is, but we should not give up our hopes.'

'If it is a challenge, we must accept it without falling to depression.

'Depression corrodes the very soul of man.'

'Like the true sons of our land; we must hunt for better roads of welfare.'

'That's right!'

'Instead, we should fight against all odds like our forefathers!'

'Fighting spirit must be preserved!'

'All should swear to serve better till the end!'

Sonba, Mahadeo, Tukaram, and Keshav
summarised their pangs and pathos silently.
Plunged into a soft debate, all those poor farmers
were searching for the dreams of sound life.
But all had a sort of fighting spirit in their hearts.
All four stopped their talk at their bus arrival.
Their appalled faces demonstrated a
supercilious pity against the system.

I thought over their talk deeply.

1 JANUARY 2013
TUESDAY

The sun rose on the village dimly that day.
The people, of both sexes and all ages failed to hold
back the tears that flowed down their cheeks.
A huge gathering of villagers, following a funeral
procession, was walking to the graveyard.
A blood-thickening moment!
Ballu Patil had committed suicide
by drowning into the well.

A hard-working and generous farmer hardly of 50 years was physically well-built and popular as a kabaddi player around a few villages. He was a commerce graduate. With all villagers he had good contacts and as by nature very natural, he looked genuinely on villagers' well-being. He owned ten acres of land. He had tried for a job in his thirties but failed. In the family of four sons and three daughters, he was fifth turn. Of the four sons, two were servicemen, one was a labourer. All sisters were married. His father, who was living with him, turned 85 and mother, who died of cancer two years ago, was 79 at her death. A sonless Ballu left his funeral obsequies to his near ones; his wife and two daughters.

VILLAGE GRAVEYARD
GATHERING OF VILLAGERS

Experts of death rituals were
humming like honeybees.
Nearly the whole village was
present for the pyre-firing.
The farmers, the workers crowded round the corpse.

'See, that's not a right direction for a man's pyre-firing?' Motiram Annaji.
'Annaji, keep quiet. We do better—you keep quiet,' Hanumant Dada.
'Is wood sufficient for this dead body?' Dasharath Mama.

'Sufficient, these are not rainy days—sufficient,'
Pandurag Tatyaji.
'Let me make it confirmed if the rockel is brought or
not?' Rajaram.
'Ask that Viju, and make it confirm?' Ajabrao.
And then they stood at the dead body.
Other expert helping hands started piling
the wood sticks on the ground.
Pyre for Ballu Patil's corpse was getting ready.
A small river, Yashoda, was almost dry.
A cliff behind the river shone pale and in front
a very good barren square used as meadow.
Only a thin flow of water could be seen at the
south bank of the slow and noiseless river.
I found myself unaccountably timid when I sat down
opposite one another on the stony ground. Hemant
gained the impression that my self-confidence was
shattered to accept the apt reality of life. But he was
silent. I was looking at the impatient pyre-making
experts how all were acting their work.
The cold breeze from north installed
a shiver in my body.
'I sometimes think,' said Kiran, my classmate in primary
school, 'that death would never come upon us,' and he
looked behind the far-reaching hill range.
'That's a final exit—can't be averted!' said Hemant.
'But, this is fairly an injustice?' Kiran.
'Injustice?
'Yeh! Injustice I would call it!'

'Acceptance of death of one's own, certainly isn't an injustice.'

'But,' Kiran advocated, 'a kind-hearted man like Kaka, when accepts death in this fashion, remains a mystery. One can't understand why and how this happens.'

'People say suiciders are timid. No, they're brave.'

Hemant made a bold statement.

'I don't consider it as an act of the brave people,' Kiran. 'See, every man fears death. So, a man who decides to meet death deliberately, don't you think it needs daring? This daring makes man brave.'

I felt Hemant was the sort of reclusive, saintly boy, who might easily have foresight.

Just a few feet away from us, a group of five was seated.

The poverty-stricken farmers!

'Do you know how it happened?' the first.

'No, I haven't any idea?' the second.

'It's a police case,' the third.

'Of course, it is!' the fourth.

'But, it is managed,' the fifth.

'No, no, not managed. Postmortem done.'

'Really? That Ramji told me, it's managed.'

'Yeh, I know it's done.'

'So why did you say, it's managed?'

'Managed, I meant dead body was brought without long inquiry!'

'It's a drowning case—that's why?'

'Exactly what happened; nobody knows.'

'It came to know late from the tongue of three workers working in the field when the dead body came up on the surface of water. It's clear that it happened four or five hours before—isn't it?'

'Reason?' the first doubted.

'Loans on head?' the second.

'No, I don't think?' the third.

'Elder daughter's marriage?' the fourth.

'But, it was fixed?' the fifth.

> The coldness longed before then
> broke out into open chiding.
> Tragic occurrence always leads
> to a blasphemous blather.
> Not knowing the reason behind the
> event could be a cruel mockery!

The sound of bells in the cattle's necks, grazing on the southern bank of the river, broke the dismal tranquillity around. The funeral obsequies were in progress. The experts were working on it. A silent, sane, humble, amiable, benevolent man and a popular farmer had led down on the bier. A good many villagers were shocked when they came to know that Ballu Patil had met his death by drowning into his farm's well when working in the field alone, the previous day. After the tragic occurrence, the villagers ran towards the field and took the corpse out of the well late in the dark. It was almost impossible to bear Ballu's death. When I saw his dead body, I was so breathless and my heartbeat so accelerated. A stunning moment it was!

'It's no good pretending he was so crazy to act like this,' I said.

'It's too sad to contemplate on it,' Hemant.

'Ballu was constantly running a tension of his daughter's marriage?' Kiran.

'Tension is the real killer of all maladies?'

'It's a very sorry state of affairs that the suicide ideation is accepted by our farmers in high degree.'

'There has started a quarrel now between farmers and other professionals.'

'I don't understand which way will be helpful to mitigate the distress of these careworn farmers.'

Our discussion was obstructed by
a group of some strangers.
It was a group of five young boys
unknown to the village.
The proceedings of pyre-firing was still in progress.

The scene of the graveyard in its broad aspect was so gloomy, even to the voices and rattle from the crowd that must be deeply felt. One tall and hefty-shouldered boy, perhaps the leader of the group, asked his companions to stand under the shadow of a babul tree. They stood just a few feet away from us.

'I am afraid these people know the fact,' the first whispered.

'I fear that somebody here would recognise your presence,' the second.

'Please, be careful about your presence,' the third.

'By the way, please be silent!' the fourth.

'Throw your fear and care for good, yaar!' he said and gazed cautiously at the crowd.

We all became cautious.

That leader boy gave fairly a suspicious insinuation of bad affair.

My mind got too much excited by his words, and the strangest fancies and surmises crowded into it.

Hemant and Kiran blinked at me with a dazed look.

'I'm terribly hurt that she left me for a tiff and defamed me. I must have to work on it.'

'Ustad, this is not a proper time,' one of his companions advised.

'No, this is proper time. The man who is on the bier now, the same man troubled me much. How can I forget him? He made a show of his leadership and barked that he won't allow his daughter to meet me.'

'She is engaged to somebody, I heard.'

'She will dream that engagement, see.'

'But, what is so special in her that you opted to do a reverse?'

'Because, she cheated me. Once she was ready to elope with me giving me a word not to break up, swore that I was fit for her and nobody will come between us; I took her to be a simple girl, but she showed her real face so quickly. No, I won't leave her,' he spoke and raised his right arm and abraded his eyebrow rashly.

'See, her father is no more now and it will be rude to—' his companion's words were then interrupted by the whisper of people.

Along with a small group of people, one leader
came there and stood by the side of a bier.
'He is the president of APMC,' Hemant said.
'I know him. He is quite a good leader of this area,' I
opined.
'Ballu was his close friend,' Kiran supplied the
information.
And then the corpse was taken on to the pyre.
All scattered people were grouped
then and the pyre was fired.
Flames of fire were soaring high into the air and
the body of Ballu Patil was burning into the ash.
In the condolence meeting, the president of APMC, Mr
Mahanoor, expressed: It's the end of the life of a good
farmer. Ballu ended his life. He was a sincere and kind-
hearted farmer and a good worker. He worked hard not
only for his family but for the welfare of farmers. We
have lost one strong worker and a dedicated farmer
today. Let us take a pledge that we will support his
bereaved family members hereafter.
It was too sad an event for me to forget forever.

FARMER THOU ART A RULER
WHO RULES OVER LAND.
TO EXERCISE AUTHORITY OVER,
FARMER THOU ART BORN.
SURRENDER TO DEATH IS CURSER.
PROVE YOURSELF A GREAT FIGHTER.

Like a wise traveller, I travelled only in search of a little place to sit in imagining myself circumnavigating a globe. I thought in my heart that there was none there to offer me a place, but I saw clearly that my attitude was nearly laughable as a girl, who was seated just at the corner of a bench, showed me the place near her driving herself to her right for making a place for me. I hesitated a little and looked at her with twinkling eyes. I knew it was very wrong spot daring to get a place for seating near the young girl, but when that girl said with courtesy, 'Come on brother, adjust here,' I dared to sit by her. I took a small notice of her. She was under twenty. A fair and fat girl. Her round face, a little fat round nose, and black short hair recalled me to think of Mamta, my younger sister. Perhaps, it was due to that girl's benevolent attitude or her solitary smile. My eyes fell on her right hand. It was covered by a long plaster. I hunted a little doubt for a fracture. She was modest.

I couldn't help seeing that she was more in trouble because of her wounded hand!

'What's happened?' directing at her hand, I asked.

'Nothing's happened!' she said playfully.

'Why this bandage?'

'What new can happen?'

'Oh, don't say that!' I said generously.

'Heaven helps those who help themselves!' she murmured.

'It's good of you to think so fairly.'

'Do you see the people over here?' she asked quickly.

'Of course, they teach us how to live!' I answered modestly.

'Yes, quite a small. Yet, they teach us more than that.'

'I understand you're very *possessive* about man's life?'

'Wrong term, brother—wrong term. I'm not *possessive*; I'm *pragmatic*,' she stressed her point.

My god, I was shocked how the word *possessive* slipped out of my tongue!

I, instantly, begged her pardon.

She smiled deeply.

'Word is sharper than weapon!' she continued.

'Exactly!' said I.

'It's not only that people teach us more; they teach us the secret of this god's earth!'

'Do you suppose the people know the *art of living*?' I asked.

'What do you mean by *art of living*?'

'This art teaches us how to live!'

'Every man knows how to live, but—'

'But?' inquisitively, I asked.

She remained silent.

I awaited her smart words.

'To my little knowledge, every man's coming on this earth is an accident?' she emphasised.

'You're accosting quite a bold statement!' I reacted.

'Might be you're right! But, I'm confirmed on my statement.'

'Accident is an unpleasant incident that happens unexpectedly or by chance. So, how can a man's birth be an accident?' I strongly interrogated.

'What my little mind understands that a very few people get a worth birth on this earth!'
And then flushing fairly, she tried to straighten her plaster-covered right hand smoothly.
I felt difficult to catch on her intellectual thinking.

'I suppose you're making a right statement,' said I sincerely.

'I think some matter disturbed you right now?' she directly asked me.

'How can you say that?' my voice faltered.

'Your face is so indicative of that—worried look!'

'Oh, worried look on face is my beauty spot!' I sniggered.

'You seemed apparently lost in thought—that's why simple to guess!' she said.

'You're a good face reader!'

'It's simple to read one's face when the face reader too sails through the same condition.'

'Oh! Wonderful! Well sister, you've learnt a lot in the small age?' I admired her quality.

'Age doesn't play a role in maturing one's personal learning.'

'Are you a college student?' I asked her.

'No, I'm a student of XII Science.'

'Reading for XII?'

'Yeh!'

'Where?'

'In this city.

'Lives here?'

'No, brother—do up and down from my village.'

I felt wrong to ask her more details of her residence. Although, of course, she was having her exchange of words like a professional lady, something in the tone in which she spoke about my worried look, gave me quite a good turn. My spirit enlivened!

'What will you do after your XII?' I asked.

'I want to join banking job,' said she involuntarily.

'Why? Your father doesn't agree with your aim?' catching her involuntary tone, I asked firmly.

'I've no father.'

'Sorry!'

'My father was a brave man.'

'How did it happen?'

'It's not fair to speak a reason in the public, I feel.'

'Right! What was he doing?'

'He was working in a private cloth store—earning very little salary.'

'Are you his elder daughter?'

'Yeh.'

'Others?'

'Two more sisters.'

'What they do?'

'The second turn is in IX and the third is in VI standard.'

'And mother?'

'She is worker.'

'How do you manage this expenditure of education?'

'I work and try to earn money for the annual fees in summer vacation and whenever time permits I go out for a work and help my mother.'

'No land etc.?'

'No, nothing of any sort.'

She sat with her right hand nervously stretched, but her face had a spot of glaring determination.

I stared at the slanting rain.
Having known from her about her father's
death, I began thinking on my father.
My heart's inarticulate cry of rage and
inquietude made me insensible.
Finding me at a meditative pose, she turned
to her left and commenced her words.

'Today's education has become costlier?'

'Yeh!' said I quickly.

'Who made it so?'

'We made it so.'

'And to run a private tuition class has become a business.'

'Exactly!'

'I'm a good learner of mathematics, but need a special guidance for the preparation of the XII exam.'

'A special guidance is impossible part—and without charge, no one will guide you.'

'Tuition class for only mathematics charges twenty to twenty-five thousand rupees.'

'Right, it's true.'

'And banking examinations rests upon mathematics.'

'Right'

'Class-teaching is a rarity in the school.'

'Yeh!'

'The mathematics class teacher of our school seldom engages her classes, instead she asks us to join her tuition class. To this day, she has engaged hardly three or four periods, but every evening we can see a queue of two-wheelers and bicycles before her palatial building.'

'It's a common scene everywhere.'

'For what these teachers are paid for?'

'For fashionable and luxurious life!'

'She comes by a posh Hero Honda City car in the school.'

'That's the *charisma* of money power!'

'But, because of their capriciousness, we are running a loss. All teachers have become idle.'

'No, no, no, my sister, that's not the matter of their idleness; that's, in fact, the matter of their attitude *plus* arrogance.'

'Who can bring a change in their attitude?'

'When I used this word, I must clear it. Sister, attitude is not a commodity which can be purchased in the market. It dwells in every man's heart as it's a way of thinking or feeling about someone or something. So, this *feeling* or *thinking* is disappearing from one's heart day by day.'

'Yeh, only *feeling* of money is alright!'

'Of course, that's the master of all human vices!' I confirmed my opinion.

'One should cry for a revolt against such vices.'

'One should mean who?'

'I mean, this young generation. This young generation has become a slave to modern technical gadgets and earning of easy money. The modern youth has no time to think over any problem like this. Sometimes their outcries are heard, but they do it for their purpose. All want money sans hard work. See, just around you, here in this public place—a bus station—and watch the style of today's life. Just watch and count the number of young people lingering here on the bus station. Isn't it a waste of man power? You'll find only disparity and disparity. The market of beggars only!' she said.

'Right, sister. You're right!' supporting her opinion, I continued, 'It's a way of life. Bad ways are very difficult to destroy. So, swim along the tide—that's the way.'

'In fact, the poor has forgotten the purpose and cause to live for,' she urged.

> Her words were so exhilarating that I
> could hardly wrench myself away.
> Like intimated friends, we talked freely
> about the present life on the land.
> The pain in my head was subsided.
> Her words sent my heart thinking seriously
> over the coming hour of my test.

'A very good talk indeed' I said frankly.

'Thank you, brother,' said she apparently.

'May I ask you about your injured hand?' I asked politely.

'Sure. I met with an accident a day ago. A boy, riding on his brand new motorcycle, dashed me from behind. Luckily, I escaped serious injury. Only a minor fracture it is but two thousand spent on treatment. Therefore, I had said, what new can happen?' she said.

'Motorisation is growing like a *congress grass*!'

'Exactly.'

'Newspapers are full of accident news. Accidents are taking place in a large number daily.'

'And resulting deaths are also more in number.'

'Life has become insecure.'

'This is insecure life on the one hand; what do you say about suicides on the other?'

'That's the grievous problem.'

'In my opinion, people know how to live, but —'

Her words were interrupted by a
loud noise of bus horn.
Silence ruled over for a minute.

'But?' I made her to complete her sentence.

'Yeh! People know *the art of living,* but they don't know *the art of dying.* Isn't it right?'

'Wonderful! Wonderful! You spoke a real maxim. Wonderful!' I appreciated her words.

For a moment she stood still, then she turned stiffly
and bidding me a good day ran to catch her bus.
Before leaving, she disclosed the
reason of her father's death.
Her father also had met with a serious accident,
but after a year died of lung cancer.
I was really awestruck for her
decent manner of speaking.

I entered home like a tremendous gust of wind.
After three months, I got back to
home and felt quite relieved.

Greatly excited, Maya and Mamta ran to me and embraced me with a humble measure of their sisterly affection. A blaze of joy and excitement emblazoned their faces. They felt my presence as a homecoming of a warrior. It was a terrible love that both sisters had shown for their brother. I was all they had in the world. My mother came out of the small kitchen, joining parallel to the same small room, and gave me a gleaming smile and a flash of her dark eyes. Bending down, I touched her feet. Stretching out her hands, she gave me a big hug and smoothly patted on my back.

> *Through her throbbing breast deeply*
> *I felt a warm of mother's love!*

'You look very weak?' she said.

'Maa, I'm well and sound! Look at my muscles!'

I gave an exact impersonation of Sunny Deol.

Mamta was too elated to say, 'Are you really at home, Dada? Daydream is it!'

Maya spread out a small bed sheet on the cow-dung-smeared floor and asked me to sit, 'Dada, get relaxed. You travelled a long distance,' and quickly ran to the kitchen.

'Mamta, how is your hand?' I looked at her and in her eyes.

'It's fine, Dada,' she said.

'Have you taken all that care you were asked for?'

'I kept every word of yours sincerely, Dada.'

'I remained very much worried about it.'

'Why? It's your teaching; never fall in care: let care fall in you.'

'Oh!' I smiled.

Maya served tea.

'What happened to my hands? Both are very good, see?' stretching her hands out, she said.

'Don't do much harder work with this hand, Mimee?' I suggested.

I called her by that name.

'It's all right, Dada. Nothing happened to it.'

'I'm glad that your understanding has grown up to this matured limit.'

'I'm not a child now. I'm as big as you.'

'I'm really proud of you, Mimee! Had I been there on the examination table, certainly I would not have performed a little bit even. But, you proved your mettle too dashingly to accord a high praise.'

'It's a part of life!'

'Mimee, how can you speak so beautifully?'

'You taught me this art, Dada!'

'No, you really are a good speaker.'

'Thank you.'

'Now, tell me about your papers?'

'Excellent!'

'Any trouble?'

'No, nothing. I had made a fine practice of writing.'

'Although you had a fine practice of writing, it would have been better to take a writer—don't you think?'

'There was a great risk on opting that. One should be confident of one's capacity. I was confident to write my papers well by this hand. I ever trust strongly in my hands.'

'My god! You're really a brave girl!'

'Thank you.'

'Now, don't care for result. It will be good, I know.'

'Good! That's not enough, Dada. You'll see my name in merit list?' her face shown a bright radiance.

My father came in.

I stood up and touched his feet.

'When did you come?' he asked.

'Just an hour ago,' said I.

I saw father's fingers loosening the ropes, trembling, face sweating. He looked a little tired.

'By eleven's bus?'

'Yes, father.'

'Today's a fine day.'

'What's special?' shrugging my shoulders, I asked.

'Your homecoming!'

He then had a bath. And after an hour, we all had a meal.

AFTER MEAL

We all sat together.

It was the last day of February.

'Mamta's examination is over,' father opened a talk.

'I couldn't come on the opening day of examination,' I said.

'How's your study?'

'It's going on, father. Don't worry.'

'To worry for children is father's duty!'

'But, I see your health is declining. Take care.'

'I'm alright.'

Mother gave a severe coughing attack.

Maya rubbed her chest and back.
'Maa is not well. Tomorrow, I'll take her to Dr Kane,' I said.
'I'm well, Babu. Don't panic,' she controlled her attack of coughing.
'We'll be doing good efforts for our health. Yours is a final year. Work and pass your examination. Mamta did her good and Maya's examination will start the next month. I want to see my children educated. Remember, there is no alternative to hard work. Acquire the aim; succeed the dream.'
My father had a dream to see his
son and daughters educated.
'I'll certainly succeed to achieve my aim.'
'And, I too!' Mamta said.
'Of course, me too!' Maya joined us.
A kind of serene fragrance made
the atmosphere divine.
Outside, the sun was climbing down the sky.
'Any problem of money?'
'No problem,' I said.
'Don't worry for money. Just concentrate on study.'
'Right!'
'Mamta did well in examination. I'm very proud of her. She won a great battle, indeed!'
'It was more than a battle, Anna?'
'Right you are! It was more than a battle!'
'She had really gone through a great test.' Mother praised Mamta.

I observed my father was never one to get discouraged. No matter how many problems and difficulties he suffered, he always looked forward to get rid of them. He believed that every cloud has a silver lining. He never allowed his heart to go wild. Entirely busied himself in work, he toiled hard for family. He was an inspired soul, really. And my mother remained his shadow forever.

AFTERNOON

*At exactly the afternoon hour, one
man appeared at the door.*

'Oh, sir!' Mamta exclaimed.

Bidding Namaste, he came in.

'Have a seat, sir,' I asked him to sit. He had carried one big poster which was wrapped in a glazy paper. He looked simple but excited. Mamta introduced him to my father and served him a glass of water. He then gave a sharp look at the house.

'Myself, Mr Paranjape, a junior college teacher of Mathematics,' he said energetically.

'Welcome sir!' I wished.

'I wished to visit you before the commencement of examination, but restricted myself.'

'Why, sir?' I asked.

'I wanted to avoid disturbance in Mamta's study.'

'Dada, Paranjape sir is one of the best teachers in the school. He doesn't take tuitions, instead teaches free of any charge to the school students. He helped me a lot.' Mamta spoke on his virtues.

Mr Paranjape was well on his fifties, a healthy man. He was dressed in his school uniform. He gave a pleasant smile and unwrapping the cover of a poster looked very gaily at Mamta.

'See, this great art?' he said.

'Excellent!' I exclaimed.

Mamta smiled.

'Mamta painted this and wrote the message in her own handwriting,' he praised Mamta.

'Really!'

We all gazed at the beautiful picture of Swami Vivekanand.

'It's not enough! See, one more miracle again!' showing a bundle of papers, Mr Paranjape said, 'see the charisma of her left hand!'

We all were greatly astounded to have a look at Mamta's handwriting.

'Simply wonderful!' I exclaimed.

'Very good!' Anna patted on Mamta's back.

'Look, Maa, look, how beautifully Mamta has written all the papers?' Maya asked Maa.

Maa expressed her joy with her tears.

'With determination and courage, Mamta win over the situation. A brave girl, indeed!' Mr Paranjape.

'I had been constantly worrying for her examination when her thumb was operated. It was a major operation and Mamta is no good using her left hand. But she achieved a summit of success,' I praised.

'Only in a shorter period of four months she regularly kept on a practice of writing and worked hours and

hours on study. She had strongly determined not to take any writer for examination, instead defeating pains of operation worked patiently to secure good percentage in examination. Even a natural writer couldn't do it but she proved her mettle. I'm sorry she lost her right thumb, a life-long loss,' Mr Paranjape expressed his praise for Mamta.

'Although it is a life-long loss, I will ever appreciate a quality in me. I must thank god for blessing me a great power to fight against the odds,' Mamta said with a strong determination.

My father imprinted a kiss on her forehead and mother embraced her with a full vigour of motherly love.

Dinner that night was a particularly lively affair on account of Mamta's win over an ordeal.

Mamta stood tenth merit in her XII standard examination, notwithstanding, her losing of right hand thumb.

COURAGE IS A GREAT VIRTUE;
PERSEVERANCE AN ORNAMENT.
SUCCESS IS A STATUE;
HARDWORK A FUNDAMENT.

It struck twelve ten in the wall clock.
I rushed into the bus station canteen
for a glass of water.

My stomach cried for food. But short money repressed my hunger. A glass of water instilled vigour in my body. Then, lifting a head up to the cloud-smitten sky, I walked out of the bus station. Silent drizzle horripilated my body. *Oh, what a chham chham barish yaar!* A *shayarana andaz* revelled in me even in that indelible condition. The road was flowing down with heavy traffic. The buses, the trucks, the cars, the auto-rickshaws, the motorcycles, the bicycles, the pedestrians were rushing in speedily, negligently breaching traffic rules. I made my way and reached the auto-stand outside close to the fencing wall of the bus station.

I stood on the auto-stand for a while.

Almost I strolled across the *chai-tapri* on the opposite corner of the road for having a cup of tea. Suddenly, one auto-rickshaw stopped on my way and I could save myself meeting an accident. *Marna hai kya— ada tirchha chalta be raste pe? Beokuf*—the auto-rickshawala denounced me derogatively. I uttered *sorry* and saving from the traffic, I rushed into the *chai-tapri*. Delving deeply into the psychology of a writer, I began to interpose myself into the small crowd sipping tea at the *chai-tapari*. Worse place indeed! But some facts should be overlooked. Having left the home, I had already determined in my own mind that anyhow annoyance must be avoided and must be kept calm. And I had proceeded to do what was urgent.

Events so far proved that I had judged
myself correctly. But my mind's other
speck rebuked me severely.
The people in front were enjoying sips
of tea, laughing, joking, joyfully.

But my tired body was interrogating me for a rest.
Joy had banned my life. Laughing had shut my lips.
My eyes rested on three boys, who were
sipping tea, standing beside me.
Drizzle lowered down.

'My father is not ready for any kind of a deal. He refused bluntly to support me,' the first boy said.

'I won't say your father is wrong, but it's the need of time!' the second opined.

'Getting service has become a strenuous job for the people like us. Monopoly reigns over,' the third added.

'Dongre, what happened to those NET/SET affected lecturers?' the first asked.

'Nothing happened so far, but some of them had filed their cases in the court,' Dongre replied.

'But, tell me Dewkar, can these peoples' cases be considered as the worth court cases?' the second asked.

'Sahare, one thing is clear that nobody would favour these lecturers,' Dewkar said strongly.

'Leave that matter. That's their problem,' Dongre.

'But the lecturer's job is a noble one?' Dewkar.

'NET and SET both are tougher examinations,' Sahare.

'After all these are examinations.'

'They all know their problems well, but aren't willing to appear for examinations?'

'It's not the question of will; rather a question of bread and butter,' Sahare insisted.

'Right,' Dewkar supported.

Nonplussed I stood standstill.
Gulps of hot tea rejuvenated my body from inside.

I thought of all my confreres who had been working in my college as contributory lecturers in various departments for the last six or seven years. Most of them had cleared NET/SET examinations. A poor lot!

'Right you are! Dewkar, I also think on this line. How can we use the word *affected* to these nonqualified teachers?' Sahare.

'I'm so confused with this word,' Dongre.

'You people can strongly criticise this matter because you're NET/SET,' Dongre nonchalantly reacted.

All three asked for a tea again.

I, too, willed for it.

'It's a useless topic of discussion,' Sahare diverted the topic.

'Let them enjoy and feed the bread of indolence,' Dewkar opined.

'My case is weak in comparison,' Dongre said.

'Why don't you clear NET/SET?' Sahare.

'But, what's the use of doing NET/SET. See your cases. You're NET/SET. But still are unemployed. What's the use, I say?'

'You're right, Dongre. I'm seeking for this job since last three years but failed to get any.'

'Sahare, you've wasted only three years but I'm wandering for the last five years. Last month, when I had appeared two to three interviews—my god, I tell you, there was a tough competition and amongst the appeared candidates most were Ph D holders and all were NET/SET holders. I've not seen such a tough competition ever, very tough!' Dewkar.

'Competition is alright. But, this bargaining—curse, really it's a curse,' Sahare.

'I heard, the lecturers are drawing lakh and fifty thousand per month,' Dongre.

'Right. Those who are placed in associate professor's scale are drawing more than that. My uncle gets one lakh and sixty-six thousand per month. Great hike in a pay,' Deokar pointed out the fact.

'And it is a welcoming job to get such a handsome salary,' Sahare.

'Sahare, after all this is an examination—alright? Is there any examination which is so difficult to get through—tell me? The result will turn into either *pass* or *fail*? But these NET/SET affected teachers haven't even tried to appear for the examinations. Instead, they are running after M Phil or Ph D and getting degrees also shortly. The failure of their will brought back a great burden upon the qualified boys like us,' Dewkar.

'Dewkar, a lot of affected ones always pelt comments on me. I bear silently. Even my principal looks down upon me. Never cooperates with me and graces me for my good work. The contributory lectureship is a painful job: little money and large work,' Sahare.

The pendulum of their conversation
swung back and forth.
Sahare's voice was clenched.
Dewkar's tone was critical.
Dongre's words were submissive.
It was clear that Sahare and Dewkar
had cleared NET/SET.

'Well, do you have any idea about the selection committee?' Dewkar asked Dongre.

'Only two names I know?' Dongre.

I looked at them with intent.

'I know all's name. But, it's not a matter of worry. All is NET/SET affected lot except that madam!' Sahare.

'But, they are doctors,' Dongre.

'XXXwar did his Ph D last year, *yaar*?' Sahare.

'And XXXkar did four or five years ago!' Dongre.

'I don't have any idea about madam.'

'Yes, madam is well qualified. She is NET/SET. And she had been to Australia for her study. She can test us all?' Dewkar.

'I too know about madam. She is a scholar coming from other University. Highly moderate person she is! She is hardly of our age but *divorcee*,' Sahare spoke a secret.

'Really!' Dewkar exclaimed.

'Yeh, I know. Bad luck!'

'What we've to do with their qualifications and personal life, *yaar*?' Dongre forwarded his view.

'We should hold our tongues on discussing such matters.'

'Sahare, yet I want to point out some different matter?' Dongre asked promptly, 'If one of us has got the chance here in this college, what will be the way of celebration?'

'My god! This man is dreaming a dream!' Dewkar laughed freely.

'Dewkar, he is right!' Sahare supported Dongre, 'Someone will definitely win the race today.'

'May I disclose one secret?'

'Secret is always meant for disclosing and thus, is fascinating!' Sahare said, 'Tell us, Dewkar, come on?'

'It may be true, but from one close acquaintance, it is known to me that one girl will get an appointment today?'

'If she is qualified and her performance is good, she must get a chance. What's wrong in it?'

'Sahare, it's not the matter of performance?'

'Dewkar, don't beat about the bush?'

'You've earned a lot from tuition classes, Sahare; but what about the small *dudes* like us?'

'So what! Why can a man waste his time in licking boots? My friend, this way is the right way,' Sahare.

'I have started taking tuitions, too!' Dewkar.

'We can earn more money from tuitions than little money earned from these jobs,' Dongre.

'It's alright, but, see forward! The Seventh Pay Commission will bring more handsome salary; what I calculated, near about sixty to seventy thousand per month to a newly appointed lecturer. And most important base is the salaried serviceman gets pension after the end of service,' Sahare.

Drizzles began to dance more
gaily after a short break.

Third round of tea made their talk more free.

'Leave this matter of senior college lecturership,' Dongre.

'That's right,' Sahare.

'It is a fact that there has been an impressive growth in the area of university and higher education,' Dewkar.

'In my opinion, we all must think over the problem of secondary education seriously, because secondary education serves as a link between the elementary and higher education,' Dongre.

'See, that is not our concern. But I always feel pity for not having a good leadership in education field. Until it is inactive, the problems in the education sector will increase day by day,' Sahare.

'To enter this area is a formidable challenge to the aspirants?' Dongre sadly said.

'In fact, I badly need a job,' Dewkar.

'I too. My two brothers are doing their education and we have no support of money.'

'Dongre, we all have more or less the same problems. I missed my younger sister's admission last year for want of tuition fees. She is now simply doing her B A in one local college?' Dewkar.

A loud thunder broke their talk.
Then they hired an auto-rikshaw and
quickly went on their way ahead.
I began to walk on my way to the college.
Looking up to the rainy clouds I babbled:
drizzle hard I deserve punishment—

*My health was adversely affected
by the cares and anxieties.
I was not in a condition even to walk. I
needed rest. I wanted a good treatment.*

But time was running out as my younger sister's admission to B Ed was due and urgently I had to arrange ten thousand rupees—just in a day. My outstanding remuneration bill was then to be deposited in the bank by the college. Eight months had been elapsed but my repeated requests to the principal were turned down abrasively. Admittedly, I was caught in the hard and the rock situation. How to lead a life in a dog eats dog world? I was running quietly across the dire situation of life. My younger sister had an urge to complete her B.Ed. as she wanted to be a teacher in junior college or in high school. She was hard-working and studious. I sincerely wanted to educate her and help her so that she would stand on her own feet and earn a salary and would get married to a suitable boy.

I reached the college anyhow.

Directly, I went to the principal's office. The peon asked me to wait as the principal was busy in some discussion. I stood outside and the peon smiled at me disapprovingly. Three lecturers came out of cabin and one of them, who was the head of the Department of Physics, Dr Bhaware, looked at me approvingly and smiled and said, 'How are you?' I necked 'fine' positively and asked the peon to convey my message to the principal. The peon went inside and came back and asked me to wait a while and smiled at me. 'Why, is somebody in?' I asked him. He kept mum but smiled wilfully. 'Ananta, please!' I urged him but what could he do.

I waited.

Admittedly, it was too offensive to tolerate
the waiting beyond my head.

Dr Bhaware came back and again went into the
principal's cabin. He left me back for a boring wait
again. Ananta stared at my pale face and amicably
said, 'Sir, you please sit in the chair there and wait.' I
sat in the chair. My eyes were aching as I had no sound
sleep for the last two days. It was urgent to meet the
principal. I was passing through such a blood-out-of-
stone situation. But it was not fair to blow my stack. I
could see only need and needy duck never cried in the
name of resentment. I had been working since the last
three years as a contributory lecturer in English in this
college and had not received the bills of remuneration
regularly. But I had carried it on like show must go
on. The slavery of man was very similar, hateful to
the body and to the spirit, to selfish cruelty. It was
apparently the class war between the slaves (like me)
and the masters: the master class. Should there have
been a peaceful and stable, healthy and high, society
until this struggle is ended? To what extend such
teachings of falsified history and dishonest political
economy and literary snobbery and abominable
scientific theory would heighten the best of all possible
systems? The laws should be reasonable and should
be administered impartially; the people should have
no way of complaining. Unemployment? At the root,
unemployment could be the real adversity.

Last year, when I had joined this college, the
principal had assured me of regular salary and had

asked me to engage extra classes as the head of the department had regularly been out of the college for various university meetings, various selection committees, various LEC committees, and so on and very abjectly I put in my sincere duties to complete the textual courses in time. But my efforts went in vain and were not amply rewarded. Admittedly, it was a useless job. I never allowed the principal and the head of the department and the students to complain and never sought any chance to say even to self, apologetically, 'I'm sorry. I'm late.' But no any concerned man approvingly recommended my hard work except the students: a real reward. I was running on empty stomach and all these people had taken me to be a safe pair of hands. But now all the scales fell from my eyes! I had to follow the way on the line of a proverb: 'squeaky wheel gets the grease.'

There was no help for it but to wait till my calling, though waiting in such a condition was almost torture to my restless, tired, and self-accusing soul. It was an act of a simple beggar and I was performing my role—a destitute in the street. Suddenly, a strange and sudden weakness descended on me as I stood gazing in the direction of the voices coming near to the office and there rushed in four strong students crying out some slogans, rashly entered into the cabin of the principal. Their leader strongly and abusively roared, 'We want money back. Immediately, we want money back.'
'What's the case?' the principal asked the leader and looked at the other three apprehensively.

'Why are you playing a game with students, sir?' the leader cried.

'I don't understand what you are saying?' the principal said airily.

'Don't understand? Okay, I make you understand. You've charged ten thousand rupees to each student as tuition fees for this academic session—right?' he said.

'That's wrong,' the principal stammered.

'Say, that's right, sir—say that's right,' he roared and other three shouted against the principal.

'No, that's wrong,' the principal stressed his words.

'Sir, you're the principal, aren't you?'

'So?'

'And still you're lying and that too with students! Don't lie to the students, sir!' he barked.

'See, I make it clear; I make it clear. We have to run the college and therefore the fees are accorded, you know?'

'Ten thousand rupees and from each student?' he pelted a question abominably.

'So, what's wrong?'

'No, sir, nothing is wrong, but it's a great offence and for that we are going to lodge FIR to the police station against the principal. Because the government's GR strongly explained to admit the backward class students without charging any fees and you have charged ten thousand rupees from them—is it not an offence?' he cleared his point.

'But, we have to run the college,' the principal again stressed the same point.

'And what about the tuition fees you seek from the government?' he pointed out his point.

'That's not the point here.'

'What's the point then?'

'We've to run other non-grantable courses also,' the principal added his information.

'Run, run, whatever courses you run, but if you don't refund our money till evening, you will see us in the police station to lodge FIR against you—okay?' he threatened.

'Let me inquire, what has happened to the office?' the principal said normally.

'You do whatever you can, but remember my words. You're playing a game against the students; you better understand,' and he sat in the chair rudely and other students again shouted the slogans loudly, 'Principal, hurrah! Hurrah!'

At once Dr Bhaware came out of the cabin and paced his steps rapidly without caring for the office.

Ananta, a lean and weak peon, looked into the cabin with eyes baffled but could not dare to go inside.

No lecturer, no office clerk or any other student came forward to defend the principal and the college was running in a full swing; the preparation of facing NAAC was on the way.

That was the tide!

'Okay, you come after a week, I'll look myself into the matter,' the principal said.

'After a week? And why?' the leader asked.

'I'll have to inquire into this matter because it's a matter of refund of money,' the principal said.

'No, a week is far too, we'll be here tomorrow to get our fees refunded, remember?' the leader said and put a paper on the table and asked the principal to adduce his signature. The principal refused to sign that paper and the leader cried loudly, 'Why don't you sign this?'

'There's no need to sign the paper. I said I'll look into the matter and inquire,' he explained.

'No, we want your signature on this paper. You do it or see the result,' he fiercely threatened.

'See, this is not fair at all,' the principal rose from his chair.

'We know better the fair or foul!' the leader said.

'See, I'm here to look after the students. I give a word to look into the matter: that's right?'

'If it's so, sign this paper,' he again stressed the same point.

'No, I won't sign?' the principal said abrasively and asked them to leave the cabin. Suddenly, that boy rose from his chair and asked his mates to break the window glasses and shouted very loudly, 'Hurrah! Hurrah! Principal murdabad!' and again moved back and angrily said, 'Remember, I'll be here tomorrow—understand, tomorrow—and will see how can't be money refunded?'

They flung the door of the cabin and walked away.

I watched their exit.

Ananta burst into the cabin.

Ten minutes passed by.

Ananta hinted me a signal to go in.

'May I come in, sir?' asked I.

'Yes,' the principal permitted dimly.

'Sir,' standing before the table I started, 'I've to talk to you. It's urgent.'

'Yes, speak,' he said unappealingly.

'Sir, I want to inquire about my outstanding salary, I mean last year's salary.'

'Salary, salary—salary? Money, money—money. I go mad. I'm mad,' the principal shirked his head.

He took his handkerchief out of his trousers' pocket and cleaned his face. It seemed that he was passing through an acrimonious situation. And I was badly in need of money.

'Sir, I want money urgently,' I repeated.

'Urgently?' he glanced at me questioningly.

'Sir, for my sister's admission, I urgently need money,' I requested acutely.

'Why didn't you try for all these days?' he asked apathetically.

'Often visits have been over, sir, for this reason,' I strongly marked my problem.

'So, what's wrong in not paying your salary? I don't understand?' he replied carelessly.

'The salary will be cleared out the next month. I mean in August—you said so, sir?' I said.

'Let me ask the clerk. You come after a week?' he said negatively and pressed the call button.

The bell rang and Ananta burst in.

'Go and ask Joshi to come immediately,' the principal ordered him.

'Sir, it's very urgent,' I again put my kind request.

'Everyone comes to me for an urgent work. Whoever thinks of my condition?' he showed his embarrassment and started looking into the files piled on his table.

Ten minutes passed by.

Joshi appeared in the cabin. He hawked deliberately and sat in the chair impolitely.

There dwelt a silence for about five minutes.

'How is this boy here asking his salary?' the principal asked Joshi.

'His salary is unpaid,' he said and waved his hand unnecessarily in his rustic style.

'Reason?'

'No funds available,' he bubbled cheekily.

'See, I said you so, often?' the principal said to me.

'Sir, one complete year is elapsed and still my salary is unpaid?' I questioned.

'So, what? It will be paid when the funds get available. Okay?'

'Sir, it's urgent. I need ten thousand rupees urgently for my sister's admission. And I had submitted my request applications for releasing my salary to the office at regular intervals. Please, consider my case. Sir, it's urgent,' I requested the principal sincerely.

'Joshi, tell him about the payment of salary?' The principal looked at Joshi.

'Sir, it's not possible to pay such outstanding amount before March. We'll try to pay his salary by March. All *contributory lecturers are to pay the last year's salary. He's not the only one and an urgent case,' said Joshi belligerently.*

All my requests went in vain.
It was strange to think that the principal was only an ordinary clerk.
Leaving the principal's cabin in utter intolerance, I strolled back to the staff room.

The staff room was almost vacant. Prof. Khade, the junior college teacher, was busy in writing his attendance register. He looked at me but said nothing. I reluctantly asked him, 'Sir, nobody is here?'
'Don't know,' he said.
'Thank you, sir,' said I and walked back to the office. A crowd of students was absent that day and majority of lecturers were on leave. There was no other way to search out any source to get money.

I really didn't know where to go?

For a fortnight after that opportunity knocked the door, I had been trying to collect money but money became more and more unreachable. At last, I decided to seek for my head of the department's help and I moved on towards his house on bicycle, suspecting that something would go right and my problem would see a pleasant feeling either and would make my younger sister happier than she had felt ever in her life. She had always been regular in her studies and wanted to attain a good job but what did she know of life's struggle :a long and bitter struggle. How long will this struggle go on? how long will this cruel wind blow and wail, buffeting me now in the back, now in the chest? Soldier, hard fighting for life! Merely a soldier! I was merely a soldier!

I moved into the main street and paddled bicycle quickly.

At last, after thirty minutes, I was at the gate of Prof. Desai's grand bungalow.

I neared the gate and suddenly a strong and stout Labrador welcomed me.

I startled a while and stepped back.

One middle-aged man came to the gate and asked me, 'Whom do you want?

'Desai Sir? I've to meet him,' said I quickly.

'Come in,' he said and asked me to sit in the chair in the porch.

For the first time I had stepped in Desai Sir's house, quite a big house! Above all, a great architectural specimen! I sat with my elbow upon my knee, considering how I should broach my need to Desai Sir. 'How pitiful it is to step in other's home for the demand of money?' I thought and tried to pacify my mind. It would be an overstatement to say that I had myself felt guilty at begging for money for a while. But I had no choice.

'Oh, you're here!' Desai sir said.

His big and brown eyes flashed a bacchanalian smile.

I stood up and smiled at him.

'Well, why are you here?' he directly asked me.

'I have some work with you, sir?' I stammered.

'Work? What work?' his voice rose to a piercing squeal.

'Sir, I am just coming from the college,' I hesitated to go straight to the demand.

'So what?'

'Sorry sir, I'm here to—' my tongue glued to the throat.

'Say, I'm here to demand money. Right?' he looked straight at me with wide open eyes.

'That's the matter, sir,' I said with my neck down.

The servant brought water.

There gathered more thoughts and feelings
in my mind as to why I stepped in there.

He went on to say: 'To demand money is easier and simpler; but return is an arduous job. A borrower is a man who knows how to borrow but shakes to know how to return. Many make a line of this type. What I believe the borrowers are the great culprits; the culprits who know how to exploit the giver's mercy and generosity. They appear sane and simple on demanding but soon change their attitude like a chameleon. Am I right?'

At that moment, I could see only my younger
sister's face, knew only one thing: my demand.

'Sir, it would be a great help to me,' I began with request, 'if you could lend me ten thousand rupees for my sister's admission; take a word from me for an early return. I will return your amount as soon as I receive my salary from the college.'

'How much is your salary?' he shrugged his shoulders.

'Fifteen thousand, sir.' I said promptly.

'And you demand ten thousand?'

'Yes sir! It's urgent.'

'You have knocked the wrong door. I can't help you.'

'Sir, I swear I will return your money soon.'

'No, can't help you!'

I stood up infuriated, dumbfounded, frightened,
and prepared myself for a retreat.
As I was about to move back from there,
I saw a great change on his face.
At once, he went inside, and coming back with a smile
on face, he put a bundle of ten thousand rupees on my
hand and said, 'Need of money can be managed with.
Go, get your work done and don't bother for an early
return.'

SUCCOUR IS A FORM OF GOD.
REACH OF IT IS A RARE.
WE HAVE TO BEAR EACH NOD
AND THINK OF FOUL AND FAIR.

My destination was in a catch.

Ahead a few steps, there was a tiny building of DDMM College. Around the place was lagged with heavy articles and the road ahead was narrow, not easy to motorise even by a vehicle. Drums of tar, big seepage cement pipes, rubble heaps were scattered along the road. Querulously, the road was groaning for a quick repair! Roads, the traffic loaders, had to do themselves in Rome as the Romans did. Suitably like a running maxim, the most wary condition here! Unlike past, the condition of the present was unscathed!

The iron gate of the college was open.

I earnestly entered the premises of the college. Muddy ground covered all over with *congress grass* welcomed me. Next, five or six dogs and a bitch saluted me with their jumping and growling. The fence of iron wires and bars protected the college building from all sides. Uneven ground and there in the right side two poles of volleyball barring net and a *babul* tree bending to the ground made everything right: a right place! Exactly in front of the building, a flagpole covered with a cement roundel was welcoming the outsiders. On the upper portion of the main building's tattered front wall, the name of the college was roaring for repainting. Two huge palm trees were swirling in an airy but rainy atmosphere. Having neared the building, I stood for a while at the flagpole, cast a look at the name of the college, and got astonished as the establishment year of the college ran 1970. So old a college! And the condition of the building was ironically sad and miserable. Hardly ten classrooms, five from the left side and five from the right side, were standing apparently. All three faculties, Arts, Commerce, and Science, were displayed on the appellation. A big college, indeed! A queue of motorcycles and three cars were parked like a ragtag. And two groups of boys and girls were swarming in the corridor.

Ditches around were laughing with full rain water.

Cleanliness was far behind.

All mess.

I entered into the corridor.

On the right side, there was an office and the principal's cabin split apart. Sultry and sulky atmosphere around! And there the interview for the post of the senior college lecturer was scheduled to be held in the principal's cabin. The President of the society, the Secretary of the society, the Principal of the college, and the Members of the Selection Committee had to arrive. So that was the condition of the college. Sitting on a bench, two servants were enjoying a talk on *satta*-market.

I went to one of them and asked about the interview schedule. 'Go there, there is your seating arrangement,' one of them said languorously and looked at me feebly. Suddenly, a wry outcry came from a boys' group on the left side of the corridor. No classes; No classes, slogans they shouted and began breaking window glasses almost fluttering with rage. No reason to understand as to why they were shouting slogans for? They stopped. Shouted again. Shouted more loudly again, and ran towards a gate.

Why were they shouting slogans?

Calmness returned back to the premises.

The servants still were resting quietly.

I went into the waiting room.

The boys, who had been waiting

for the event, looked at me.

Clearly, I observed those three whom I had seen at the *chai-tapri*. Sahare, Dewkar, and Dongre threw a sangfroid look at me. All right! I sat on the bench. The uncleaned room smelt badly. Humid and wet atmosphere made it rancid. Effluvium everywhere! All those boys had come in wearing very good clothes on. All had good-quality bags with them. But their care-smitten faces were telling me the story of their struggle. The decrepit job seekers like me!

Unemployment sacked the life of youth!

I tested my shirt carefully and it angered me. Repeatedly, it was worn for the last four or five days, and over it the dusty bus travel! Patches of dirt could be seen on it and the trousers also needed washing. Who had time to wash clothes? I had been always out of home. Could only two good dresses afford the need? Poverty thy name is adversity. I never had attended any interview for the last six years by having such dirty clothes on. Reluctance won't work then! One should be very punctual about dresses while attending the interview and the college. One must be—that's right! I kept my file on the dusty desk. On the wooden blackboard, some dirty captions were written. Definitely by the students. But no servant or any good student would have made an effort to rub off that mischief. The walls of the classroom were also painted with rubbish words and some stickers and colours.

Then two more candidates entered the classroom. A boy, who was in his best crimson shade shirt and jeans trousers, and a girl, who had stylish and trendy jeans trousers and tops on, sat down on the front bench and smiled at me casually. Having taken one heavy book out of her bag, she began to turn over the pages. That boy spread a concerned look at every corner of the classroom and muttered some words to the girl. I could catch with my careful eyes that that was the same boy who had attended the interview in one college last month. Egregious smartness had covered his face and he seemed very confident. He had ridiculed the system of NET/SET examinations in his discussion with me. He was doing his PhD under one of the professor's supervision, yet he could not clear NET or SET examinations. I dislike these bogus examinations: he had shown his dislike.

I closed my aching eyes; badly needed rest.
As that girl sat there, looking at the blackboard, she must have her moment connected with a thought felt before! She was beautiful and looked intelligent and shockingly her face was found to be very similar to Sarita! Only the height made the main difference.

Sarita threw me back to my college days.
Yeah, golden days!
DARKNESS DARKNESS DARKNESS
Imagining myself a strong feathery
bird, I soared high in the sky.
There echoed Sarita's sweetest words in my ears.

DECEMBER 2005
SATURDAY

'What a big heart you've got, my father! Can you tell me from where you've adjusted money?'
The house had scarcely recovered from grim economical sensation and the events of the next few days were piquantly muddling to each and every member of the family. I felt guilty of having no way to earn for the family. Still I had to complete my post-graduation. Before accomplishment, one shouldn't

draw the long bow. My father in the heart of his heart wished me to be an educated person. He desired to look me in the authoritative chair. He always felt extremely uncomfortable whenever he saw me in any petrified situation or in any danger; he looked after me so scrupulously that it couldn't be removed from mind. Lovable and lordly man! A man of big heart!

'Why did you come so urgently, father?' adoringly I asked.

'You needed money, urgently,' he said.

'But, it could have been managed anyhow.'

'Why anyhow? Money and time are invaluable.'

'But, you're not well nowadays?' I looked at his pale face.

'My wellness is all my children!'

'This is my last year, Anna. My hard work will amply be rewarded.'

'That's my prayer to god!' He put his hand on my head and kissed my forehead lovingly.

'How is mother?'

'Well. Don't care. See only the target and aim it. Time runs fast. Catch it. Conquer it.'

'Mother's care makes me worried.'

'Worrying for such worldly cares is human's frailty. Health and care go hand in hand.'

'I feel guilty for giving you and mother trouble,' meekly I said.

'See, the time ahead is very competitive, stern, and thus one has to leap in the dark. Aim is like an arrow.

It has to be perfected! And after all, the life is a whole rigmarole!'

'Well, father, I won't allow my concentration to divert from my aim! I'll attain the goal!' I said confidently.

'Don't waste your time now in family worries. Reap the sweet fruit of your hard work, it's ahead!' he said and looked up at the sky and walked out towards the bus station.

I stood leaning against the pillar until my father was out of sight.

Thus, day by day, five months passed. Only five months were in hand. And the final year examination; my god, anyhow, the percentage must be secured. Two hundred rupees? My father gave me only two hundred rupees? And I had to manage with all my efforts the purchase of important book on Dr Radhakrishnan and the charge of mess. My father looked worried and his body showed the signs of soundness dying away. 'Ever, forever, I live but for you, I will work hard for you,' I sang the lines of my own poem for him.

I reached the college late.

I had to extract notes on literary criticism.

I attended only two periods and directly went to the library and I sat by the window and sadly watched how the earth kept exhaling atmosphere, thus air blowing coolly and then immediately made myself busy in extracting notes on literary criticism, my favourite subject (but had a strange fear for it). Hardly an hour had passed, I was interrupted by Sarita bursting through the library door in her usual fashion, as though she had discovered some strange matter of life and said in a gush of energy, 'Come, we will have tea in the canteen,' and energetically walked to the door without waiting for my reply.

> *The golden sunlight pressed through the
> window and flashed over my face.*
> *Softly without a sound, I followed her in
> a mesmeric fit as fast as I could.*
> *UNIVERSITY LIBRARY CANTEEN*
> *Down we sat.*

All that day the cold was normal. The sun was travelling to setting. Its golden tint touched the tops of tall palm trees and gulmohor trees and bougainvillea plants and the bird cries went up into the crescendo. Hurriedly, I put a book on the table and opened my words: 'Shall we depart immediately after tea?'

'Why, so early?' she said alluringly.

'Hardly five months to go for an examination.'

'Yah, but you've no problem. You're very regular in study,' she said and smiled adoringly.

'Time is a great task-master: Milton said. Time will disclose our result. Why boasting before a successful end?' I elucidated.

'It's all right, but some relaxation is also urgent.'

> *She ordered for coffee.*

'No, tea is enough!' I said.

'Coffee is preferable in these days,' she said and looked through the window. 'You look quite nervous today.'

'Nervous? No, I'm worried for the criticism paper,' I cleared.

'That's really my case also. It's very difficult for covering up the percentage in criticism paper.'

'Aristotle and Coleridge are tougher to understand, in my case.'

'But I'm afraid of that biggie question—practical criticism.'

'After all, it's a difficult paper,' I said and looked at the door.

Father's pale face dashed an awakening call.

Harishankar, the waiter, put the cups of coffee on the table and looked quite wishfully at me and smiled.

'Do you feel the teaching-staff of this university is competent enough to teach the subject like criticism and even modern literature?' she forcefully remarked on the teaching staff of the English Department.

For a moment or two I had no answer.

I marked a glaring sense of pride in her eyes and her swinging gesticulations are far too bold!

But I found it very pleasant and immediately seconded her opinion. She finished her coffee. I waited by myself for a few minutes. I could think of nothing but Sarita and her bold and catching style of conversation, almost like an expert commentator! Never had I dreamt even to have such a nice talk with a beautiful girl like Sarita! I thought in my heart that there was none in the dreamy life of mine to equal her, but at the same time, I saw quite clearly that my attitude was comic, irrelevant, ridiculous! In fact, I was entertained by her mesmerising beauty and gracious presence, but was it not an act of building a castle in the air? It was difficult for me to take my eyes off her as she was certainly a most beautiful and attractive creature and that too was very difficult to understand why was she spending her time with me behaving as if she was apparently in love with me?

Strange! Strange! Very strange thinking!

'Robert Browning is much more difficult than Tennyson, don't you feel?' she waved her words.

'Nothing is difficult. We make everything difficult— either it is literature or life.'

'The good part is I am aware of my punishing routine and still there are chances.'

'Listen with your heart and not just your ears; see things will smoothly go on.'

'Path of disinterested action is difficult.'

'When we forget the original saga, the difficulty arises.'

'Okay, may I quote the lines of one beautiful poem, if you lead to interest?' she asked.

'No, it's late today. I came here only to return your book and that too on your asking. Thanks!' I said.

And I rose up from the chair.

'Please, sit for a while and listen to what I' m going to quote. You'll surely like these lines,' she asked me.

A sort of a deliberate purpose sparkled in her eyes.

'Okay, say then?' I said benignly.

She recited.

Be a god and hold me
With a charm!
Be a man and fold me
With thine arm!

Teach me, only teach, Love!
As I ought.
I will speak thy speech, Love!
Think thy thought.

'*What do you say about these lines?*' *said she as if apparently lost in thought.*

'*This is pathetic and lovely,*' *I concluded my opinion.*

'*Do you recollect from which poem these lines have been extracted?*' *she asked.*

'*These are from Robert Browning's poem titled 'A Woman's Last Word,*' *said I confidently.*

'*Will you, please, explain the meaning?*' *she asked.*

'*There is gentle pathos in these lines. The woman in the poem decides to merge her identity in the will of her husband and to this end she merges her intellect into her heart. But there is an almost oppressive intensity of womanhood. This much I can explain,*' *frankly I said.*

In her look I could calculate an equal amount of amorous feelings.

From her beatific expression, I could not help feeling convinced that she had some loving inclination towards me. I felt very sobered in her company. Her face, her eyes, fresh smile, her words, I liked by heart.

We left the canteen.

BUS STOP

The great masses of golden-colour clouds smothered the sky and broad beams of sunrays shone through the clouds. The sky was beautiful and clear. And under the sky when I walked with her, a strange flutter there was at my heart. I felt the time was running very slow as I wanted to have her company. I stretched out my hands in an ecstatic joy to the sky and the lines instinctively played on my lips: my heart is beating, keeps on repeating—

She might have observed a change in me?

Oh, she was too pleased to see me delighted!

'Today I see a joy under your sorrow!' she exclaimed.

'Oh, no, I'm sorry. I'm late?' apologetically I murmured.

'But, it's evening now. We have to wait for a bus.'

'We missed the five o'clock bus?'

'The next is at six. Wait!'

Down she sat on the bench.

I stood by the light pole.

'We're only two today, waiting for the bus!' she looked at the library building.

Taking out her costly mobile phone of her expensive purse, she tried to connect some number.

A few minutes passed by.

'My mother is a busy person,' she said.

'Is she employed somewhere?' I asked in anticipation.

'She is a senior college lecturer,' she said, elegantly brushing her soft rosy cheek in her own smiling style.

'And father?'

'He is deputy collector,' she said, proudly pulling her beautiful lock on her forehead.

'And brother or sister?' I asked.

'No brother and no sister. I'm their only daughter.'

'That's good!'

'But, I felt for a brother!' she said very frankly.

'Why not for a sister?' I asked, but amicably.

'One son, one daughter, proves a good formula for a happy family,' she said and looked at me.
'Right!'

Sun sank to rise again.

WAITING FOR BUS

'Okay, what's your opinion about John Donne's philosophy of love?' she diverted the discussion.
'I've just started a reading on him; so can't explain clearly,' I emphatically said.

Awakened I stole my look at her.

'Whatever I have read, I didn't find much difference between Donne and Browning,' she said promptly.
'More or less same, but the only difference is of their age and personality, I think?'
'What do you understand by personality?'

Her eyes reflected a strange sense!

I never had seen such an amorous look. Her glaring face was showing mysterious signs of attraction!

SENSUOUS!

'—' I spoke no word.
'Yes, say something on personality?' she continued.
'What I know about the word is—personality means the qualities of a person's character that make them interesting and attractive and in other words, we also can say, the various aspects of a person's character that combine to make them different from other people.' I tried to explain the difference exactly as it is given in the Compact Oxford Reference Dictionary.

'So, what do you find in my personality?' she wittily asked.

I smiled.

Her beauty was beguiling.

I paused. I was lost in thought.

'Okay, will you please distinguish between "beautiful" and "attractive"?' she shrewdly diverted her words.

'It's difficult for me to distinguish between these words?' changing my posture of standing, I said.

'Try, at least!'

'Frankly speaking, these are not the words that a boy like me can explain.'

'But these are most common words!'

'May be, but very difficult to explain.'

'Do you feel upset in my company?' she asked overtly.

'Don't misunderstand me,' I said sincerely.

'What about today's coffee?'

'Nice!'

'Hasn't it got a taste of friendship; good friendship!' she smiled.

Her words were too difficult for me to explain.

But in the heart of my heart, I thought in full that the time would stop and the bus would never come and she would never go, would never depart. She would speak for a long, long time, smiling, laughing! No, no, of course, that talk and that waste of time, that had nothing to do with my condition, especially my poor condition. I felt my heart was wrung with such a spasm that I could have roared out and her face troubled me moment by moment. She had joined my department *just four months ago and tried to come in my contact whenever she got the chance, always avoiding the company of her girl classmates. She was rich. She knew that I was the topper in the class. That might be one of the reasons why she wanted my company. She was an interesting girl after all! But for me, the world was a vale of tears and the suffering that life brought! A mere farmer's son couldn't be a Vicar of Bray? Wake up call! Yes, her approach, intimacy, company, and fondness for an acquaintance, certainly had a cause, but it must be a wake-up call for me?*

How could a down out boy long for a
rich and beautiful girl's love?
I might call it love either?
BUS ARRIVED
We departed.
Why did one feel strangely different at night?
The wintry moon also seen sad that night!
That night I dreamt a terrible dream!
I woke up late in the next morning
with a strong assertion to read for
examination seriously and sincerely.

LOVE IS MADNESS, LOVE IS GRIEF.
FRUITS OF LOVE ARE ALWAYS BITTER.
LOVE IS FANCY, LOVE IS ANGUISH.
LOVERS FALL IN ITS SWEET TEMPER.

Outside it was drizzling.
WAIT WAIT WAIT

Uttered the clerk a loud cry entering the classroom.
'*Yeh*, how many are you all? One, two, three—six? But seven are there on the list? One is absent? All right—absent means no headache! Good, shortened list. Better! Come on, come, one by one—*karo apni apni sayana karo—yahapar*—on this paper? Soon interview will start.'

I adduced my signature on the attendance sheet.

My turn was fifth.

Six candidates had to appear for an interview.

Six candidates and my turn fifth.

The chances of selection: almost bleak!

WAITING

Tossing and turning thoughts ascended on me.

I felt little disturbed at that time.

what can be asked—what type of questions—easy or difficult—on literature or grammar—criticism or trends—writers—studied—for examination—knocking—disturbing—the mind—no special criterion—for asking questions—whatever—whatever—can be asked—depends upon—inquisitors—but—their mood—last year—december—interview—nagpur—interview—attended—tough—tough interview—real testing—of knowledge—and—selection—on merit basis—really—some—institutions—go—for—merit—what—happen—today—no—no

One lady peon brought a tray of tea cups.

O, my god! My face sparkled with joy.

I badly needed tea.
Hungrily, I took up a cup and tasted tea.
Little quantity, but poured consolation.

HOME HOME HOME
MAA MAYA MAMTA

—now—it is—half-past-one—time—over—all would have gathered—would have done on time—waiting—must—have been—waiting—such cases—time—important part—immediate decision—needed—alright—no—people—help—in such conditions—people—in village—good—helping—they know—remedies—know—solutions—setting—things right—but—about—me—about—only son—cries—cries—been spread—remarks been splashed—on—been pelted—on—what's—in hand—no way back—carry on duty—that's right—tingle—again—tingle—mistake—mistake—incorrigible mistake—been made—today's time—unavoidable—never—will come—back—for that—today's interview—search—of—bread—butter—for—family—how—could—been avoided—what wrong—done—don't think—don't hope—here—zero chances—selection—doubtful—who asks—bare man—poor man—moneyless—baseless—unsupportive—like me—many interviews—many experiences—merit—achieved—first division—m a english—net—set—cleared—still unemployed—travelled—travelled—a lot—spent—big money—all wasted—here also—what guarantee—despair—despair—despair—delusion—depression—bitterly— been avoided—today's importance—must—been followed—son's duty—unnecessarily—hunted—more value—to interview—know—know—well—decision—be taken—by brain not—by heart—but—wrong—decision—'m wrong—really wrong—seen—only—one side—of—event brighter side—remained dark—left unseen—what's—that moment—deceptive moment—life—time—brighter—darker—brighter—fainter—but darker—chaos—dilemma—mirage—cobweb—made—made—ghastly mistake—torture—pain—grief—me—till—end of life—agonising moment—sheer absurdity—summit of insensitivity—philosophy—reality—all fishy—inhuman deed—death—death—no alternative—death—final exit—death—immaculate—immutable—horrible—death—terrific—*to what we fear of death*—mere—words—everybody—fear—*death be not proud*—philosophy—*when i have fears that i may cease to be*—can't—work upon—death—philosophy—is philosophy—death—death—certain—final—horrible—poverty—curse—strife—life—is struggle—iron will—poor man—fighting cock—fight—for—daily bread—father—father—iron will—fight—end—end—conundrum—problem—convulsion—mother— save—me—your rage—deserve—punishment—blunder—but—loss—permanent—quagmire—no—way—loss—loss—loss—

LOUD HUBBUB OUTSIDE

I came out of the classroom.
Rain still was on the go.
Tiny drops of water could be seen falling down
from the inner face of a slab of the porch.
The entire corridor was looking like
a newly wedded dark lady.

Outside at the end of a tattered fence, the *babul* trees were stuttering a gleeful song of rain. And the scattered *congress grass* was enjoying water to grow more. The office staff was busy in the work, but a loud noise made the air harsh and huffy. The principal of the college had yet to arrive? Wait was the only way in hand.

1.30 p.m.

A long wait made me irascible. Weather also was not supportive in any way. Wait? But how far? I walked two rounds of the corridor, my eyes lingered on the office. There in the porch stopped one motorcycle. One short and bonny man ran to the corridor and hurriedly rushed into the office. Soon he came out and shouted, 'Mhadeo? O, Mhadeo?' One middle-aged man came out of the extreme corner-room of the building. 'Mhadeo, go and stand there in the porch. Pratapdada is coming. Go, hurry! Go,' that short and bonny man asked Mahadeo almost twisting his body. Mahadeo went and stood in the porch. That short and bonny man took one round of the southern corner of the corridor and rushed into the office. Mahadeo looked very scornfully at the man, who just had rushed into the office. *'Noutankii saala!'*

he blurted and spit on the floor carelessly. He looked at me and smiled without reason and again raved, '*chalati hai; noutanki karate, saa—ley!*' Noticing Mahadeo's deliberate contempt for the man, who had rushed into the office, I moved up to the classroom. Mahadeo's scornful look and contemptuous behaviour made me ponder over the proletariat attitude.

TEN MINUTES PASSED BY

Three cars stopped in the porch.
Cautiously, I looked at the people who
were coming up towards the office.
There came two men in the corridor.

One of them was a lanky and languid man, dressed in white shirt and jeans trousers, who made his first impression by spitting a strong torrent of *pan-pik* in the porch. He cleared his mouth with a dash of left palm and looked at the office airily. The other one was a dark complexioned, tall, and tough man, who seemed careless to all situations, which was apparently revealed from his gestures and a way of walking. He was dressed in long *kurta* and *pyjama* having left a thick gold chain out round the collar of the *kurta*, as if to model gold ornaments. A pompous man, indeed! Both of them approached slowly to the corridor. A lady, in a navy blue colour *saari*, carrying a file close to her chest, followed them.

Hurriedly, that short and bonny man (*he was definitely the principal of the college*) came out of the office and welcomed those three with a flattering smile on his face and moved his hands acrobatically for no reason. The madam and the principal went into the office. But, those two lingered in the corridor.

Quickly, that lanky boy, Dongre, whom I had seen at the *chai tapari*, came out of the classroom and ran to them. The first man spit carelessly again and, coming forward, said to Dongre, 'Have you brought a copy of degree?' His highly standard pronunciation made me to laugh! Rustic tone! Leaning to his feet, Dongre said, 'Yes, sir!' The man said, '*Okay, badme bolata mai—?*'

And they went into the office.

SNEAKY FILMY SHOT

I was about to move back, there I saw
that lady coming out of the office.
Quickly, she went to her car.
She came back.
'Sarita!' exclaimed I.

SARITA SARITA SARITA

My completely flummoxed mind
railed back to my college days.

25 DECEMBER 2007
CHRISTMAS DAY

For me it was an indiscreet journey.

Often in the past I had wondered what it would be like to be subjected to some unhappy but great trial, more agony, more pain, more suffering, more exploitation, more persecution, notwithstanding, I had longed for affliction. That day I was much caring for my result of NET examination but my mind was filled with a startling burst of energy ardently hoping to get through the examination. I had a bad habit allus to toss the coin for catching the desiring result; an ugly way of trying luck, a fooling act! Round and round, I went with that tossing and made my mind confirm on my result. Excitement made me forget all my past pains and I reached the University Office to see my result. I flung out my arms in excitement and in a lavish gesture when I saw my roll number in the result sheet of successful examinees. Tears stood in my eyes; I was glad. I was happy. Elated, I came out of the office and looked up at the blue sky and thanked heaven for His blessing! I saw my security and stability in that result as I had achieved a great step of competition.

Suddenly, a gentle voice came on my ears from my back and I stopped. 'Hey, stop a little?' Sarita came near and with her alluring smile congratulated me. 'What a nice girl she is!' I thought. I smiled gaily at her and danced my steps towards the university campus canteen. 'Let us celebrate this moment with your favourite coffee, Sarita!' Looking deeply into my eyes, she followed me. I was too elated to celebrate that moment that day! I never had dreamt so great and passionate company of a beautiful girl; a moment proposed to me by heaven.

On the tea table, she opened the discussion.
'I feel bad I didn't appear for this examination.'
'I insisted on,' I said and ordered for the coffee.
'That's right,' she tossed her costly mobile phone and again expressed the words of congratulation and looked very amicably at me.

With filtered emotion, she neared
her hand towards mine.
I felt myself a handsome and a
romantic figure that moment!
'You're very good,' she said.
'Thank you,' I replied.
'A very enjoyable event for me too! Thoroughly, I want to enjoy a lot,' she said.

Her words had a deep meaning.
She smiled gracefully.
ECSTATIC MOMENT
She was dressed in moderate garments and
looked extraordinarily mod and beautiful.
In a frenzy of delight, my soul
touched the seventh heaven.
My eyes grew bright. Amorously, I
felt for her lovely company.
Was it a dream! Wasn't it true!

I felt I had pushed my face forward—and—and—imprinted a kiss on her rosy lips—one little kiss—a kiss—on her gleeful cheeks—made me forget everything—so heavenly—made me immortal—never—never—never—

How could I!

Dream of a poor soul!

'Now the real struggle has started, you know?' she carried on.

DREAM SHATTERED

'Exactly!' I opinionated.

'We spend very beautiful days of our youth in such arduous journey across the sea of problems?' she said and lifted the cup of coffee up to her lips, her favourite drink.

'But happiness never comes from anywhere! Man has to dream long dreams and has to sort out gay from very difficult problems and odds. Who dare not embark upon such journey, always jump into the gulf of sensations and destroy life? Life be taken as a toy; play with it, play, play, and intoxicate it,' I claimed my opinion.

'Your words are so fascinating!' gaily she said and finished her coffee.

'Jesus said, "When we see beauty in each thing of nature, we become happy but the first condition is how we adopt to look at everything with highly positive thinking."'

'Is only positive thinking enough?'

'Positive thinking and right action go hand in hand,'

'This is a very sad year for me.'

'Why?'

'I tasted only defeats this year,'

'What do you understand by defeat?'

'Didn't appear for NET or SET examinations.'

'Is it a defeat? How can you take it as defeat without appearing for an examination?'

'But a sad ending of year, 2007.'

'Sad ending never asks us to carry only on a dreamy path; dreaming only to fill in all happiness into the pan of honey and one can't taste it.'

'How can you speak such beautiful words?'

Affectionate glee reddened on her beautiful face.

'Time is a great teacher. Time teaches all things.'

'Wonderful!'

'Have you read any writing of Amrita Pritam?' I fondly asked.

My eyes centred on her face.

DERRING-DO ACT

'No, never!' she replied.

'You must read in spare time. It's an experience to learn something from life, really,' I supported.

'You're very poetic in your words!'

'Everybody is a poet of life! And must be a poet who could well sing the pangs and pathos of life!'

'Hence, the poet's life is always sad?'

'Sad because the people think it so suffering!

'And why should a man accept suffering?'

'Because in it, we can see the image of god!'

'And what about love?'

'Love is that madness which all lovers have?' firmly said I.

'There is rapture on the love shore?'
Her cheeks were brightened with
roseate glow of dawn.
'But it's like a pathless wood?'
Forwarding my straight opinion, I observed her
glowing face(sheer oblique attack on her face).
'My steps are not upon that path yet, but I dream to
ornament it with my loving waves. I've to see what
human things can do. I've to lie on the bank of a deep
sea of love, and having drunk exceedingly the nectar of
true love, I wish to drink life to the lees!' she elucidated.
She took a deep breath and calculated her long
and soft fingers as if she were in a long dream.
Her face turned into a glorious mirror to
watch in life's miraculous adumbrations.
She appeared to be a girl walking in beauty!
Her eyes reflected so soft, so calm, so passionate, yet
eloquent tinting glow that would charm even the dull
human being!
Could I see with full soft emotion the
shades of appealing true love for me?
Could I see serene and pure expressions
of love in her dark and deep eyes?
Could I observe so excellently fair and beautiful face?
Although my path was rough and tough, the joy
within me dallied with distress—all madness!
With groans of smarting wounds in heart,
at once I retreated on my real path.
It was a dream dreamt by me the broad daylight.

I paused, held my breath in a long silence, and boosting up man's prime vigour into the heart, hardly I could speak a few words on love as she required me to speak, 'Love is nothing but a poet's sad song?'

SILENCE

'A man who is caught in Hamlet's query 'to be or not to be' dared not go along the path of love as child simply dare not go in the dark, am I right?' she said.

'I recall Shakespeare: a lunatic, a lover, and a poet are the men of imagination all compact. One sees more devils than vast hell can hold, that is a madman; a lover, all as frantic? See Helen's beauty in a brow of Egypt: and I frankly tell you Sarita, I fear for life!' I tried to authenticate my views.

'But, life can be too different altogether,' she said.

'Let us depart now,' I said.

And I rose up.

'Why so early? You're now a relaxed bird!' she smiled.

'Relaxed? No, this is only a step ahead on the way of struggle?' I cleared.

'Well begun is half done; you always say.'

'That's right! But I'm not a relaxed bird; caged bird you can say?'

'Okay! Shall we go to the Devi's temple today?' she tried to ascertain my will.

'But, it's five kilometres away from here.'

'Yes, I've my activa with me. We will have Devi's darshana, today.'

On a drive to the temple, my mind was haunted by thousands of penurious natural shocks, apprehending some joy in shamed and hateful and fearful life. Weary life under sweat couldn't permit anybody to drive on the way of love or anything of such a luxurious way! Man should lead a life with purpose. And love certainly could not be a purpose of my life? I must keep my mind in control? I must follow a Japanese maxim: 'fish's decay starts from its head.' I must keep my head calm and confirmed on such issues. Sad soul you are!

After all, Sarita's case was different.
She was rich enough to enjoy life in any way.
But I must walk on my real path.
I had my own entrances and exits and had to play many parts: son, brother, and a few others.

LOVEMAKING IS A FOOL'S ERRAND,
MANY TROUBLES CROSS ITS PATH.
I MUST USE HARD MEASURES TO IT;
I MUST PICK AND CHOOSE MY EXIT.

2.00 p.m.

Level-headedly, I tried to scrape off the past.
Mahadeo, a very interesting man,
came back in the corridor.
One posh, black Honda City car, stopped in the porch.
Mahadeo ran quickly to the porch.
Mahadeo opened the door of the car.

One tall and strong man with a high belly (*must be the president of society*) came out of the car stylishly.

A good-looking middle-heighted man (*must be the secretary*) followed him. That short and bonny man, the principal of the college, ran towards the car and welcomed them. Having taken a round of the corridor, they discussed some matter, had a round to the southern end of the building, and then quickly went into the office.

Silently, I entered the class-room.
2.30 p.m.

INTERVIEW INTERVIEW INTERVIEW
TIME RUNNING FAST

ordinary college—no value—for time—time of interview—1.00 p.m.—now—it is 2.30—bafflement—chaos—restlessness—fear—confusion—mind—what—will happen—what will be the result—who will get selected—interview—my god—no normalcy—no hope—under such condition—interview—tension—mounting on—specific tension—altogether different—hallucinating effect—condition like—*macbeth*—but—tension—bleak—chances—bleak—almost—bleak—idea—tension—corrupt—one's knowledge—dark—dark—darker—recollection—becomes difficult—tension—harmful—no—fear—fear—kills soul—harms confidence—no tension—fear for result—fear for selection—groundless—baseless—usual process—anybody—everybody has—chance—can be selected—hope—shattering

of hope—weakens—ambience—hope—the best—
wait for result—tension—tension—but how—can
it—be overcome—no—tension—much smaller than
necessity— important—look forward—look for
bread—hunt for butter—father works hard—day in—
day out—burns blood—sweats harder—wears away—
for family—limited income—limited sources—limited
money—burden—burden—loans—insufficient—
problem—asks for marriage—my marriage—33 years
son—unmarried—no way—no hope—secure bread—
no choice—marriage—oh—that lady—hundred
per cent—but—that madam—*sarita*—definitely—
sarita—my classmate—now—must be married—
her—no—that boy—was—if—it's true—divorcee—
my god —terrible—must not—come upon—her—her
proposal—not at all possible—poor has no choices—rich
girl—deputy collector's daughter—bride of wealth—
thatched hamlet—my poor life—no—right—she went
on—right path—now—senior college lecturer—*phd
holder*—*net/set*—on selection committee—my god—
time—runs faster than will—face interview—under
her—how—baffled—baffled—how to answer—her
questions—problem—known person—is—difficult
to face—and—*sarita*—my god—a fly—in the
dip—*katherine mansfield's fly*—special—extremely
special—interview—for me—new—episode of my
life—testing—poor boy's testing—will she—recognise
me—if—what will go—further—my state of mind—
my appearance—my study—my knowledge—my
confidence—what a maze—selector—her right—will

ask definitely—merely candidate—appearing for interview—what a situation—but—no odd thinking—should not—why should—but—difficult—very difficult—situation—and—why should—she—be careful—about me—selector—she is—selector—care for candidate—am i special—am i privileged—one—no—she won't care- mustn't be—other selectors—ready with their armaments—how to cut—how to kill—they all know—killing is their instinct—selectors always find—way —to catch—mistake—they try—to grab—opportunity—how to dominate—boys test—of knowledge—but few—are talented—scholar—well knowledgeable—many—shallow—with—scanty knowledge—rough knowledge —no command—over subject—merely come—for show—on—selection committee—very lucky—people—handsome salary—handsome life—beautiful wife—smart children—flat—bungalow—car—estate—and—what not—limited work—least responsibility—least botheration—least care—worriless for time—only—how—they shallow—don't bother—for—the last six—years—'m trying—an interview—vast experience—still—'m doubtful—and—can't guess—what—can be asked—struggle—is on—and—yes—call me—vainglorious—call me—bold—call me showy—or whatever—tell you—my experience—tells you—so many—lecturers ask—difficult questions—try—to test— candidate's knowledge—but—in reality—are they themselves—able to answer—those questions—last year—one question—was asked on—*mahatma gandhi's autobiography*—and—the selector—*net/ set*—affected—but—*doctors—phd holders*—eulogised—*mahatma gandhi's english*—said—*mahatma gandhi*—used—highly beautiful sentences—in *english*—in his—autobiography—tell me—is his—autobiography—really—written by—*mahatma gandhi*—in *english*—fact is that—*gandhi*—had written—his autobiography—in *gujarati* language—and later on—*mahadeo desai*—translated it—into *english*—but—the selector—on the basis of—his wrong knowledge—tried to dominate the candidate—see the situation—want performance—and basically—they themselves are wrong—and height is that—in one of my interviews—i met such a lecturer— who had brought— written list of selected questions—with him—while asking—questions—he repeatedly -- was looking into the list—and he was—the subject expert—they deliberately—try to confuse the candidate—try to over-show their knowledge—try to confirm their intelligence—many examples can be cited—about the lecturers—who are mediocre in knowledge—but are on the salaried posts—drawing salary of one lack rupees—and more—per month—handsome salary—but ugly knowledge—performance they want—now tell me—how many selections have been done—on performance basis—calculate the percentage—hardly two or three—in one hundred—my guess—because of—this poor knowledge in the subject—the passing percentage of *net/set* examinations—is hardly—two or three per cent—why then—government agrees to that—but -- won't cry for that—what's the use of such crying—useless—set up—everything—goes on—systematically—necessity demands some sacrifice—necessity is necessity—need is need—necessity makes—me—steal need—desideratum—closely associated—with me—and patience—resolution—forbearance—all needed—these—be made friends—all these—will show me—a way to overcome—the present situation—these are my—right friends—my best friends—this will be—my real strength—'ve to fight out—in life—on the dint of inner and outer strength—real struggle—struggle neck to neck—be *ullyses*—be fighter—be warrior—empowered with—odds and odds—worries and worries—struggle and struggle—this is—my travel—and how—can i rest—from my travel— like *ulysses*—*'m a part of all—that—i have met*—otherwise frustration—no—*made weak by time and fate but strong in will*—fate—no—i said—fate is— scary—word—will guffaw—hard word to meet with—gives challenge directly—to heart—directly to soul—defeat leads—the way to success—accept defeat—remove fear—lodge courage—persevere patience—n win over—fortune—traveller—'m traveller of life—very complex—very intricate—like a cobweb—don't know— way out—situation makes—man more dawdling—more passive—but no—this is—not the end—walk alone—win the race—father—you taught—me—how to fight—strive—

From the corridor, there resonated a
loud call for the first candidate.
The first boy, Dewkar, cautiously checked
his bag and stood up for his move.
3.00 p.m.
Coming out my doleful delirium, I
cautiously positioned myself.

SWEATING SWEATING SWEATING

I cleaned my face.
Dewkar rushed into the cabin.
I calculated the time and made
myself ready for my turn.

ANNA ANNA ANNA
Father! O, my father!
True son of the soil!
May I be a winner?
Great, I am the dreamer!
Father, thou are a great fighter!
Thou art a soul rose up from out
the dark clouds of struggle!

I lulled in the heart of my heart, my father cared for
me much. His vigilant eye kept me safer from ugly
habits and vagabonds in the village. He inscribed a new
definition of a caring father in my life. A great soul!

Anna's advice: Inflation does not cause a problem; deflation causes more. My statement is bold but right. Farmer is a person who falls a first prey to deflation. The low prices of food-grains pave the way to corruption. Criticism is welcomed to my little thoughts. Ever I think on my fellow farmers' attitude towards life. Why do they easily surrender to death? They lack in indomitable will and single-minded dedication. They never take into consideration that a kite flies against the wind and not with it. They walk on the way disheartened, instead they should work hard to overcome the hard situation with double vigour and greater effort avoiding casual way of surrender. Mind it well my son, strong will alone can win the war. Remember the words: the man who wins is the man who thinks because to think is to feel responsible. Son you are born a farmer's womb; love your land and achieve success by right way and right thinking. Bless you success!

After fifteen minutes.
Dewkar came out of the cabin.
On the second turn, the short but healthy boy amongst those three, Sahare went into the cabin. And then, in his sluggish walk, the peon entered the classroom with a list in his hand and slightly coughing cleared his words, *'How many are you re!'* and having counted the number of present candidates, he went out.

And at his exit, I began to flow down
with uncountable thoughts.

—boy went just now—looked confident and cautious—gestures and expressions—could be observed—*dewkar* looked somewhat embarrassed—shall—i go to him—and—ask—about his interview—who asked—and what type of questions—he was asked—by the selectors—*n*—yes—*sarita*—oh no—*sarita*—losing confidence—paves the way—to divert—from—solid status—that— must be—relish with— expressions—solid behaviour—time of interview—before facing interview— after facing interview—congeals blood—but that boy—*dewkar* sat calm and quiet—seeming now—very different—than his earlier appearance—secret—yes secret—must be there—waiting—what for—why—not gone—stayed—secret—waiting result—might be—or—he been—asked to wait—or because—outside rain—hardened momentum—which category—he belongs to—post for open—category—might be of—open category—but—who can leave—the place until the result is heard—happens—many time happens—management asks candidates to wait—became part—of interview—nowadays—no reason—to doubt—no reason—to think over—but here—two methods apply—one—asking candidates to wait—until selection is done—on the performance basis—or—that's important—asking select candidates to wait—until interview is over—second method—is applied—when there is—complete bargain—if bargain is already over—then—it remains mere formality—mere feigning—nowadays—second method—is on the verve—*dewkar*—is waiting—reason must be there—shake doubts—come out—come—be normal—be attentive—

Amongst remaining, the third boy on the list was that verbose boy, who was harshly speaking against the NET/SET holders; an ordinary boy having least command over language, but very rustic in manners and very ugly by nature. Unsuitable candidate for the job of a teacher! He stood up from his place and hesitatingly went out of the classroom. Waiting was making me irresistible. Wait! The competition was just bare; no special talent had been seen so far as it had been in Nagpur last year, tough and healthy competition. *The competition must be there. The competition brought to us readiness and punctuality, sturdiness, and thirstiness. The real test persisted through the tough competition. Knowledge in the subject must be tested and tossed. That would be the essence of competition. Toughness made the way of life more prosperous and punctilious. The great way adopted and followed by the great people turned them into the greatest in the world*—I thought to myself.

The third candidate went out of the classroom
and stood up resting his back on the wall.
A mere confusion was gathered on his face and he continued to look at his wristwatch. How vaingloriously he had criticised the education system and peoples' scholarly approach? And how wrongly he was speaking? Incorrect pronunciation, incorrect knowledge, and

stupid attitude and a wrong way to criticise people? But how he had looked embarrassed and disturbed then? Ordinary and careless approach always brought us difficulties and it hindered mind from aim. But his nasty habit of chewing *kharra* made him costly ugly. Tension was certainly mounting on his face. Tension of interview or tension of bargain money? Guess was difficult?

Wait Wait Wait
Nearly after fifteen minutes.
The second boy, Sahare, came out.
And the name of the third boy was announced loudly—Amol Kawale. I came to know his name. He toddled to the cabin with every step full of fear. Tension of interview had caught him full. He disappeared in the cabin and I became worried about result.
My turn was the fifth.
And that girl's was the fourth.
Still to wait at least for forty minutes!

responsibility—severe—responsibility—only—son—responsibility—surmounted on me—responsibility of—home—five members—and—expenditure—survival—money—question of—bread *n* butter—responsibility—is price of greatness—said someone—but 'm i great—drops of thought—spattered—door of home—again—two o'clock—time—went—over—time never admit—any mistake—blunder was committed—rain covered all area—rain—rain—everywhere—how could have been done—by the people—how could have been adjusted—no facility—no wood available—no other facility—what mother could have done—not the duty—of woman—needed man—man's duty—all would have stopped—all must have been waiting—small river—in village—great question—fast problem—but had made—mistake—n interview—that final—this final—no this was—not the final—could have been attended—next time—but—that is—final exit of life—won't come again—took decision by heart—not by brain—but—great dilemma—sad—sad—sad—what remained in hand—tears n tears—could be flowed down—but—what meaning in shedding—never admit—pain—never—grief is grief—magnification of grief wrong—lamentation heightens grief more—gratifies more—but present—is present—should be given priority—my thinking—what about people—what about relatives —what about society—what about villagers—what about uncle—what about mother—what about sisters—what—what makes—maze—all will crush—me under blames—will criticise me—my qualification—my wisdom—my knowledge—my duty— all will fall prey—to harsh criticism—against society—against traditions—against society rules—against society ways—poisonous words—will welcome me—harsh banters—will be showered—upon me—but—done over—no way back—avoidance useless—mistake—incorrigible mistake—in search of bread—hunting for bread—can be mistake—sincere effort—is putting in—even then mistake—opportunity never strikes—door again—opportunity once lost—ever lost—grabbing opportunity—great—divine work—utmost duty—*n*—who brought any chance to my door—who will bring service—to my hands—will service come automatically—to me—six years—strenuous work—continuous efforts—travel—travel—travel—expenditure—all—who helped me—how then service—would come to me—who is behind me—who is—god father—is there any—is there anyone—closely associated—any *mla*—*mp*—or any *minister*—no backing—no support—more experience—only support—broken—lost—no standing—but a problem—only fight—struggle—struggle—but—no—surrender to struggle—fight on—fight—won't like—word luck—what is luck—mere surrender to—indolence—no surrender—only—to fight against—the circumstances—whatever—previous night—stormy night—father—storm came on—before—time—strange—fit of—time—no mercy—of time—open field—pathos—pangs—loss—irreparable loss—*dude*— thou art lost—lost—lost—

My thoughts were broken by the
silent voice of Sahare.
I looked, with my heavy eyes, at
him and tried to smile.

'Oh, damn it! It again started *yaar*!' watching the light drizzle, Sahare exclaimed.
'Nature's mood!' uttered I.

'But, it is unnecessarily disturbing all!'

'Out of man's control!'

'But, I must go now?'

'How was your interview?' I asked directly without caring for his reaction.

'As usual! Didn't feel that am facing interview! Ordinary—most ordinary questions are asked. Nobody was interested in asking questions. Asked me my name 'n address 'n city 'n village—and summed up. Is it an interview?' Sahare disappointingly elucidated.

'Why didn't they ask questions on literature or language?'

'*Arrey*, not a single question? Doubts rose in my mind, whether these selectors can ask questions or not? Whether they're qualified or not? Only name, father's name, surname, address, date of birth, and NET/SET certificates—finish. And to tell these silly answers— came from such a long distance—expending money, wasting time, and tiring body. Shit! Sheer foolishness!' Sahare thumped his right hand on the wall.

'Oh, sorry *yaar*!' I begged his pardon.

'Sorry, for what? You'll also come to know their foul game soon! Selection is already fixed *yaar*!'

'Oh!' I sighed.

'Are you NET/SET?' he asked.

'*Yeh*!'

'Fine!'

'Are you, too?'

'*Yeh*!'

'I doubt somebody is already fix?'

'So, no use to attend and waste time?' I said.

'Try your luck; if you are here?' he said and sighed.

'Trying luck is merely madness!'

'In these days, madness is also granted as wisdom. We are between the devil and the deep. So, dash in.'

'Fine words!' I exclaimed.

'Actually, we're not facing a real competition here. We are just six. Dongre is not qualified and others—that girl and a boy—don't know about them. And even if they are qualified, the competition doesn't heighten a problem. Because only five candidates doesn't prove a tough fight? If the management and the selection committee really opted for selection, one of us must get selected. And I frankly tell you, my candidature is already subtracted. So, real fight remained amongst you four. That's why, I said, try your luck. Right!' he forcefully expressed his opinion.

'Thank you for your suggestion,' said I.

I tried to read his face as I was reading a
legal document between the lines.
I must confess that at his words a doubting
shudder passed through me.
Sahare, then, walked slowly towards a water
tank silently singing a line of a filmy song.
And I continued my wait with
every nerve on the alert.

On his coming back, Sahare went to Dewkar and spoke some words with him. He looked quite nervous.

'Okay, friend, I take a leave. Passing time here is kicking against the pricks. Best luck. Good-bye,' he said.

Soon he left.
Amol Kawle had come back.
I again came back and sat on the bench.
Pranjal Mankar—the peon roared a name.

A girl, who was still reading a book, stylish and snobbish, smart and soignée, hurriedly stood up from the bench, making her modern dress neat and correct. She came forward and asked me, 'Please, will you keep an eye on my purse? Okay!' and she went out. She was Pranjal Mankar. She looked very elegant in her modern dress. She rushed quickly into the cabin.

I just came at the door and looked
anxiously at the cabin.

The lecturer, who had enquired of a degree to Dongre, came out of the cabin and taking him to the west corner of the corridor involved in a secret talk. What was the secret? There must be some? Their talk continued for five minutes. And then, Dongre came to the classroom.

I was still standing at the classroom door
keeping my eyes on Pranjal Mankar's purse.
Dongre stood beside me and looked
suspiciously at me—spy's eyes!

time—time of—my turn—interview—coming near—next—number—turn fifth—somewhat—secretive atmosphere—around—that boy—*Dongre*—nervous—looking—at me—suspiciously—why—the girl—*Pranjal*—went—just now—will be—back soon—is she—qualified—what preparation—what

reading—no—she was right—she was reading—
continuously—since her arrival—preparation
must—*n*—what—can *i* do—for preparation—have
no time—all wasted—in homely matters—over this
disturb—melancholic—condition—mournful—
sad—sad—very sad—this anxiety—curbing heart—
worry—what next—don't know—time coming near—
fifth will be—me—sixth—that boy—*Dongre*—my
turn—my turn—will be—questions—too bulky—
history of literature—thousands of writers—short story
writers—dramatists—novelists—poets—critics—
essayists—long—long list—all buzz—in mind—all
strike—mind—*anglo saxon*—*chaucer*—comes *n*
says—stylishly—o man—don't forget me—*i'm* father
of poetry—can't go further—without me—avoiding
me—first honour—mine—'m father—old *english*—
father—*spenser* dashes—like strong bull—says—in
stunning words—'m poet—of distinction—my place—
in *english* poetry—is like—guiding star—my *fairy
queen*—simply excellent *n* classic—no comparison—
at all—donne—metaphysical poet—*death be not
proud*—cried he—*n*—sacrificed—life poorly—but—
will say—nobody—can't forget me—no *elizabethan
poetry*—is complete—without me—awaken boy—*i*
came on—stage—in fifteen ninety-three—when—gale
of *elizabethan poetry*—was completely blown—itself
out—*n*—there was—chill in—air—definitely—he
will cry—he—tried—tried—*n*—submitted life—
like—angel in the clouds—*n*—man *n* poet—*n*—
dramatist—par excellence—that—great—great—

great—*shakespeare*—poet *n* dramatist—of all ages—
roars—like lion—can any selector—go forward—
avoiding me—can—syllabus of—any *university*—be
completed—without my inclusion—'ve you—gone
through my *hamlet*—my *lear*, my *macbeth*—my
othello—my *julius caesar*—n my heroines—study
more *yaar*—study more—concentrate on—my
heroines—my worthy lady characters—*desdemona*—
ophelia—*rosalind*—*calpurnia*—n—still more—
all will—perch on head—*n*—silently—*milton*—
comes—gives—challenge—if able—any reader—any
scholar—ask questions—if not—forget me—but—
mind it well—dare not—to murder—my spirit—*n*—
in reality—ninety five—percent lecturers—scholars—
readers—don't even touch me—in better words—
torture me—*i* don't tolerate—mistakes—laziness—in
my study—*dryden*—comes—his *alexander's feast*—
dwells in mind—roars he—his reputation—comes
from—reasonableness—elegance—suavity—of
his verse—*wordsworth*—sings—in his—natural
style—romanticism—his pantheism—his theory—of
poetry—smoothly—he enters—into mind—poetry—
spontaneous overflow—of powerful feelings—
oh—what—theory—*kya baat hai*—right you're—
right—but why—this boasting—right—you're—*mr*
wordsworth—right—but—that friend—your friend—
that opium eater—*samuel coleridge*—very—very—
powerful critic—powerful poet—*coleridge's* poetry—
is challenge—mediocre readers—difficult—very
difficult—to understand—his poetry—theory of

poetry—*jonson—shelley—keats—byron—tennyson—browning—arnold—hardy—dickens—lawrence*—*n*—many more—list—long—long—no end—many more—'re there—one thing—be kept—in mind—kind of—relaxation—very—few lecturers—read literature carefully—do not study—new writers—don't care for—to know—new trends in literature—why—should they—they—'ve to teach— compilation—text book—of prose *n*—poetry—some eight—nine poems—of hardly fifteen lines—*n*—same number—of lessons—of two three pages—some items—of grammar—which 're already—taught in—high school classes—middle school classes—all 're not ready—to teach some more—in literature—think that—criticism means—*aristotle n eliot*—*n* it is limited—to these critics—only—no selector asks—new *n* current critical theories—*n* trends—*n* movements—modernism—movement—post-modernism—structuralism—post-structuralism—feminism—eco-feminism—protest literature—subaltern literature—post-war literature—*n*—what not—my god—no rest—unending list—of writers—*n*—trends—*n*—movements—but—very interesting—very outstanding—should be asked—on current trends—*n* movements—real testing—of knowledge—real parameter—seek—great pleasure—on asking—scholarly questions—*gabriel garcia marquez—salman rushdie—albert camus—franz kafka*—must be—there—in—literature study—pity—no such testing—in interviews—selection committee—*n* university—seldom appoint—lecturers—competitive enough—on

selection committee—but—why should—*i* grudge—
my grudge—my opinion—my views—valueless —
there is—selection—but—not on—merit basis—only
on—material basis—money—money—money—

After just ten minutes, Pranjal
Mankar came out of the cabin.

She sat near me.

Sighing deeply, she took out a water-bottle of her purse
and drank a few gulps and turning to me said in a silent
tone, 'Literature is a very tough subject? How can a
little mind store so vast a knowledge like a computer
chip! My god, I'm saved! Are you the next?'

I necked '*yes*'.

'Are you Net/Set?'

'*Yeh*!'

'When did you clear it?'

'Both the examinations I've cleared in 2007.'

'My god, both, and that too a long back?' she said with
surprise.

'I've just cleared SET last July. And now I'm doing Ph
D under Madam Sarita.'

'Fine!'

'Very tough interview.'

'Who asked more questions?' curiously I asked.

'The principal and the VC's nominee,' she said playing
with her smart-phone.

'And ma'am?'

'Two simple questions only.'

'Good. You're escaped the test. Mine is the immediate
turn.'

Then she hurriedly went to the office
and had a talk with Mahadeo
Her words made my mind think more on the event.
Mine was the next turn.
Innumerable thoughts started scrapping my
confidence and threw me into the pond of ennui.

my turn—interview—time strikes—now—*sahare*—
right—are there—any rules—for success—no—*i*
don't think—if—there are—any—unless man—
works or does—for it—sitting still—wishing for
good—merely—makes—no man—successful—
worry—worry—worry—is—interest—paid on—
trouble—before—it falls—due—so—why—bother—
event—of any kind—must—be faced—simply—this
is—interview—right—

agree—there was—cause—why—it—be avoided—
certainly—cause—but—had—it—been avoided—
it—would have been—more kicks—than—half
pence—what—*sahare* said—must be followed—
candidate—fixed—he said—but—doubted—may
be—true—bargain—it's—business—has to draw—
further—trapping—prey—has to be—enunciated—
money grabbed—money earned—systematised—
labyrinth of—progress—management—pile sums—
of money—esquire money—in the—name of—noble
cause—of education—no values—no ethics—
nonchalantly deterred—*n*—what—cause prevailed—
money—be accentuated—future—of—human-
being—money—money—money—mirthless—let—it

go—should not—shudder—should not—shatter—
will—confidence—right—confidence—needs—inner
strength—inner strength—needs—strong soul—my
father—advised—my father—is it—right—to stop—
here—no—no—stop—*i* won't—stop—but—must
retain on—own decision don't think over—to avoid—
interview—avoidance—will be—another mistake—
deliberate—waste of time—*n*—shaking of—
responsibility—no—no—no—glue to—decision—
Anna—Anna—Anna—mercy—mercy—mercy—

A sudden long ominous bark of a dog
shattered my reverie and I awoke.

TEN MINUTES SWOOPED AWAY

But there sounded no roar for my name?
Outside, drizzles were weakened.
O! Sirimiri!
Mahadeo, this time, came at the door and
marking on the list said, 'Hey! Number five?'
I uttered, 'Yes!'
And he broke loose, '*Badhiya hai!* Seven number *apsent*.
After you there is one more. *Mamala khhattam!* Finish!
Tuesday. Ghatsthapna Day! Durga Devi's Day! And I'm
here? And this much work upon me? No holiday? Work,
work, and work! *Saala,* no life for a common man? No
private life; no enjoy! No wife, no *balbacche*! And no
good salary? *Chhut!* Hey, you, stop for a while. Wait
some time. *Saab, bade saab,* 'as an urgent work—many

works he 'as to do. Just came from America—*bade saab*! Going. Stay. Now your number—*khallas*!'

Mahadeo went quickly into the office.

SURPRISING! SURPRISING! SURPRISING!

It was very surprising for me!
Secretive cobweb hampered me.

—president—going—meaning—interview—finish—importance—finish—my turn—without—president—what—value—useless—meaningless—or—some—purpose—might be—candidate—fix—useless—sahare—was correct—waiting—unimportant—waste—time—wasted—why—wait—then—better—to leave—quickly—no—importance—my—turn—no—value—president—is going—got it—very meaningful—fix—candidate—is fix—all clear—no meaning—in interview—why—stay now—better—to live—quickly—bargain—all the way—*i'm*—not—in race—it's all clear—*i'm* not—minor figure—even in—their big calculations—money—money matters—number five—*n* six—meaningless—but number six—is not—qualified—only—me—remained—prey to—malicious—foul play—moneyless—worthless—meaningless—by all means—meaningless—*n* lo—left—home—for meaningless job—curse—curse—upon me—o, god—pray—don't save me—don't protect me—curse me—punish me—big culprit—bigger culprit—biggest one—no mercy—no redemption—punishment—dirty—disgusting deed—'ve

done—*n*—for this silly thing—mere hopes—to me—no
one here—my deed—hopeless—my wish—sinner—
sinner—great sinner—

A muddled state indeed!
I came out of the classroom and stood
up at the pillar of the corridor.
With feverish look, I gazed at the dark sky nervously.

Vain look. Vain wish. Vain hope.

After ten minutes, the peon dimly cried my name.
But my resilience quantified back aggressively.
Little hesitantly, I trudged into the office.
The office was most ordinary.
Hardly one could call it an office. No maintenance. No
cleanliness. No synchronisation. All roughly arranged.
Tables of the clerks were arranged on both the sides.
Four clerks were seated in their chairs. One of them was
busy in computerising some data on his computer. Five
to six tin cupboards were set in a row.
All seemed lazy and careless.
There in the corner of a joint cupboard,
one black cat was resting.
On my passing, it flared its bewitching yellow eyes.
Ominous look!
And it mewed.
Its silent mew accelerated my heart's palpitation.
CONTROL CONTROL CONTROL
My confidence, my determination, bounced back.

And with determined steps, I entered the
cabin asking, 'May, I come in, sir?'
That short and bony man said 'Yes!'
Coming forward, I wished all.
All were busy in some discussion.
Only that short and bony man looked at me and said,
'Sit there!'
'Thank you, sir!' I said.
He was the principal of the college.
The centre chair was vacant.
(*The president had just gone out somewhere*)
'Take your time and test the candidate,' the good-
looking man, who was the secretary of the society, said.
'Right, sir!' the principal said.
Next to my chair on the left side,
that madam was seated.
Now it was clear.
She was Sarita!
Her ravishing black eyes, fixedly,
widened a steady look of my face.

HOW FAST TIME SPEEDED BACK

Lovely fragrance of past could be smelt in the air!
But how could I face her look?
'Yes, tell me your name?' the principal asked.
'Sir, my full name is *Ajay Vithoba Kanade*,' I replied.
'Your date of birth?'
'My date of birth is 22nd July 1983.'
'Your caste certificate?'

'I have already attached it to my application, sir.'

'You belong to reservation category?'

'Yes, sir.'

'Your mark list?'

'It is also attached, sir!'

'You brought all your original documents?'

'Yes, sir,' said I, and showed him all original certificates.

'Your percentage of M A?'

'I secured 65 per cent at M A.'

The principal calculated and checked
my percentage carefully.

Next to my chair on the right side, the dark complexioned man was seated. He rolled his fingers on his gold chain stylishly and asked the principal for my file. Having taken a careful look into the certificates, he looked at me rather abominably. He seemed abrasive.

'Are you merit?' he asked.

'Yes, sir! I stood second merit in my MA examination,' I answered promptly.

'NET/SET finished?'

'Yes, sir. I cleared NET in 2007 and SET immediately in 2008.'

'Taken one year and say immediately?' he smiled quite abusively.

(He was VC's nominee who was asking me questions)
I remained quiet.

All others, except madam, looked at me analytically.
Madam seemed between the devil and the deep.
She then turned to me.

*(Her almond-shaped eyes reflected
measureless emotions!)*

'Are you employed somewhere?' the madam asked.

'Yes, ma'am! I'm working as contributory lecturer in KKVR College.'

'Why didn't you try for a permanent job?' she asked.

She then hopefully fixed her eyes on me.

'For the last six years I've been trying, but come away empty from my efforts,' I answered.

SEE MY FATE SARITA

My mental feeling was so curious.

Just for one moment, I was anguished.

WHY WHY WHY

'What college said you?' the lanky and languid man, who sat next to the dark complexioned man, asked.

'KKVR College, sir!' I repeated.

'NET/SET—both finish?'

'Yes, Sir,' I repeated.

'Caste certificate? Not here?'

'It's there in the file, sir, on number five,' I said politely.

'You are NT (*pronounced as en t*). Wants open category.'

Looking at the secretary, he stressed on his question.

(Very difficult question!)

His abrasive stare made me aggressive.

'Can't any backward class candidate appear for an open category post, sir?' I asked strongly.

'Whatever asked that much answer only,' he reviled in a boastful voice.

(Enjoy the language of the subject expert!)

'What is the long form of NET/SET?' snarled he in his robust tone in reverse.

'Sir, the long forms of NET and SET are National Eligibility Test and State Eligibility Test, respectively.'

'What is the difference between NET/SET?'

'Sir, by and large, the syllabi of both the examinations are same. The only difference between these two examinations is : NET is conducted on National Level, whereas SET is conducted on State Level.'

But, my explanation failed to satisfy him.

'I want,' stressing on his words, he repeated the same question, 'actual difference.'

'Sir,' I continued my explanation to make it more clear, 'National Level examination is related to All India Level and State Level is related to State Level means Regional Level.'

But again he nodded negatively.
There must be a machine for studying
a mind system, I felt.
In fact, it was quite a well-known
form of man's behaviour!
He, stealthily, took out a piece of
paper of his shirt's pocket.
And then the president came back
and sat in his centre chair.

'What is your favourite form of literature?' he then stylishly put his question.

'My favourite form of literature is *short story*.'

'And what about criticism?'

'I like imaginative literature, sir.'

'What is criticism?'

'Criticism is a study that deals with the critical assessment of literary or artistic works.'

'Who are modern critics of literature?'

'I A Richards, Helen Gardner, Cleanth Brooks, Robert Penn Warren, Richard Hoggart are some of the important critics of modern literature.' I tried to list the critics.

'Who wrote the book *Criticism as Pure Speculation*?'

'Sir, the critic J C Ransom wrote this book.'

'What is *Vorticism*?'

'It is a literary and artistic movement based on *Cubism* which was founded by Wyndham Lewis.'

'And what is *Futurism*?'

'It is a twentieth century movement in Italian art, literature, and music promoted by Filippo Tommaso Marinettti.'

After cleaning his face, he paused.

(*Undoubtedly, he was reading a
prepared list of questions*)

He, then, tossed and turned about,
and blurred in mouth.

'Ask Xxxwar, sir,' turning to the dark-complexioned man, who sat next to him, he said, 'Ask. You are VC's nominee.'

Xxxwar sir made his seating position right.

He coughed lightly.

His drowsy eyes sparkled as if he was heavily drunk.

And having played with his thick golden
chain, he blurted a question.
'Can you say something on the Georgian Poetry?'
I discovered to my relief that that
wasn't a difficult question.

'Sir,' I continued, 'the Georgian Poetry is an amalgamation of several trends of poetry. The tendencies like a scholarly tradition, Catholic Movement like that of "Metaphysical Poets"; an aesthetic tendency as an impact of Pre-Raphaelites; a tendency of Realistic Impressionism based on acceptance and Naturalistic Reversions etc. are easily and strongly noticeable in the Georgian Poetry.'

'Who coined the *phrase* Metaphysical Poetry?' he continued.

'Sir, the *term* Metaphysical Poetry was coined by Sir William Drummond of Hawthornden in his letter to Arthur Johnston in 1630,' I answered quickly.

'What? What name you told now?'

He looked at me in an acute bafflement
like the embattled general.

'Sir,' I repeated the name of the author, 'he was Sir William Drummond of Hawthornden.'

'Oh, Mr. what name you are telling me? That was Dryden?' he grumbled.

His face showed complete disapprobation.
Only the madam felt something.
Slowly she raised her eyes and looked at me.

'No, sir, he was William Drummond of Hawthornden, a Scottish Poet who coined this term in 1630 and it was first applied by Dr Samuel Jonson in his *Lives of the Poets* to certain poets of the seventeenth century, but the real inventor of this term is taken to be John Dryden, who used this term in his *Discourse of English Poetry* in 1690,' confidently, I cleared my answer.

Surprise embezzled with disapproval
blackened his face.
The secretary seemed very much
pleased with my answer.
But the madam headed positive
response on my affluent answer.
Xxxkar Sir, the subject expert, looked little disturbed.
There fastened a silence for some time.
Taking an expensive golden-coated cigarette-case out of his blazer's pocket, the secretary like a sudden torrent galloped out of the office.
TIME OVER TIME OVER
'Madam, ask your questions?' the principal swabbed in style.

Madam was quiet.
Might be for the situation forthrightly occurred there.

SILENT INGENUOUS LADY
SCHOLAR INDEED
FOUR EYES TWO FEMININE TWO
MASCULINE TOYED TOGETHER

Trying up her beautiful locks, the madam
began in her solemnly elegant (*known*) style.
'Well, from your mark-sheet, it's clear that you offered
American Literature. Will you, please, define the term
Expressionism?'
'Expressionism is a German Movement in Literature
and other arts, especially visual arts, which was at its
height between 1910 and 1925 that is in the period just
before, during, and after the First World War. It is the
writers' or the artists' attempt to express inner feelings
and intuitions. The expressionist playwright presents
the condition and working of the mind of his characters
and wants to show their anger, sadness, sorrow, faith,
sacrifice, etc. The expressionist's theme is man's
psyche. What is a stream of consciousness in novel, is
expressionism in drama. A little attention is paid to the
form. Dialogue too is not realistic. It employs dramatic
devices such as soliloquy, heightened language, asides,
masques and pantomimes, chorus, suggestive scenery,
costumes, lightening, sound effects, etc., for giving
outward expression to thoughts and characters.' I tried
to explain the definition.
'Very good!' affluent remark rose from the madam.
But all others except the president
could not bear out my answer.
Clouded displeasure on their faces was
enough to disclose their negativity.
The principal ran his hands through
his oily hair and smiled casually.

The strange half-smile came and went upon
Xxxkar's lips as though he lived by dreaming.
The Head of the Department scurried
towards the office door.

DAWDLING MINDS DILLY-DALLY OUTLOOK

The secretary came back.

'By what name H W Longfellow and J R Lowell are called?' the madam continued.

'Both the poets are called *the Bramhin Poets*,' I answered.

'In which of the dramas, Eugene O'Neill experimented a *stream of consciousness* technique?'

'Ma'am, Eugene O'Neill experimented a *stream of consciousness* technique in his play titled *Strange Interlude.*'

'There are three terms—Mulatto, Quadroon, and Octoroon. To which people the term *Mulatto* refers to?'

'Ma'am, the term *Mulatto* refers to the people who are *Half White* and *Half Black.*'

'Who wrote the book *White and Black* on the struggles and persecutions of *Negro*?'

I thought a little.

'The book *White and Black* was written by Herbert Sand and it was published in 1922.'

At that moment, I could clearly watch
a glowing face of the secretary.
The rest of the committee members, except
madam, showed undignified consolation.

Why were those two Xxxwar and Xxxkar so stodgy? Suddenly, the longest, most intimate look had passed between me and the madam as if two of us had said to each other.

'See, my next question is on grammar. As a teacher, you will have to teach grammar in the classes, all right? So, tell me the meaning of a phrase *to begin the world*,' the madam caught back the momentum again.

Indeed, the question was very hard and competitive.

I came up with confidence.

'Ma'am, the meaning of the phrase is, *to start in life*,' I explained.

'Right, quite right!' she said and immediately put the next question, 'will you please, use this phrase in a correct sentence as you are going *to start in life*?'

How strong the lavenders (*the past*)
smelled in that marshy wet room!

'At present every man needs good quality education *to begin the world*.' I answered quickly.

'Very good. My questions are over,' said the madam.

The principal turned to Xxxwar Sir and asked him, 'anything more?'

'No,' said he.

But the head of the department, who had sat calmly all this time, turned to me and dashed his question. 'Tell me what is the difference between *this* and *that*?

'Sir, *this* is used as pronoun and determiner—'

Interrupting my explanation, the head of the department, laughingly said, 'I said tell the difference?'

The president asked the head to keep calm saying, 'Let him speak. He started a very good answer.'

'Sir, as a pronoun *this* is used to identify a specific person or object close at hand and as determiner, it is used to mention period of time specially related to the present. *That* is also used as pronoun and determiner, referring to a person or object seen or heard by the speaker. The use of *that* is difficult because there may occur confusion between *that* and *which.* If a clause gives additional information, *which* is preferred to *that* in a sentence,' I tried to explain.

On the president's accord, the interview
was summed up at last.
Greeting all, in an utter state of
confusion, I came out of the cabin.

While trotting to the classroom, the head of the department followed me, and said in abhorrent words, 'Ye, boy! Kanade, stop outside and don't go. Come when called in?'

Out I stood for a while.
Complete exhaustion. Complete confusion.
Complete doldrums.

I needed water. Acute thirst had made my throat dry and hoarse. I walked towards the water tank. I stopped at the plasto water tank kept unkemptly in the southern corner of the building. A dirty place, indeed! A 500-litre plasto water tank and below it the two plastic taps! No stand. No glass. Opening the tap, I leaned to drink water, but the tank was empty. Oh! My god! Water, too, had vanquished me! Water! Water! Like a defeated soldier, I walked back to the classroom. A man who sat on the stool at the door of the classroom looked at me and surprisingly asked, 'Why waiting? Because of rain?' I had no answer. I kept mum.

'Please, give me a glass of water, uncle?' I said. The man reluctantly rose up and went into the office.

I quenched my thirst.
I took a few deep breaths to calm myself down.
But my mind was running relentlessly.
A high confusion, surmounted by Sarita's
presence, had blocked my mind.

SARITA SARITA SARITA

Stealthily my mind entered into the past.

24 MAY 2007

THURSDAY

After clearing NET, I had made myself busy in the preparation for interviews. And for that I had made a schedule, but things didn't pan out according to schedule. Another big war was waiting for me. I felt I didn't much want to waste my time in trivial matters like visiting others. I thought I wouldn't meet anybody that

*knew me and it was pretty silence there. If there was one
thing that I hated more than another, it was the act one
had of disturbing me on the study table. But suddenly,
Sarita appeared there. Exactly, five months later, I was
meeting Sarita in the University Library. It was almost
a surprise. I couldn't hide a joy on my face. And I must
admit that I didn't sleep well during that period without
recollecting a beautiful face of Sarita dreaming very
high of her memories.*

Sarita smiled elegantly.

Outside it was very hot.

Then after a few minutes' travel, we sat in the garden.

*I knew, Sarita did it deliberately and
she had some purpose on doing it.*

Disconcertingly, I looked at her.

*She read a discomfort on my face and opened her words
gracefully, 'leave that Shakespeare and your reading
aside for a while! Keep yourself calm and pleasant. We
will have a nice talk today. Come on!'.*

'Sarita, a long way I have to walk up, you know?' I said.

*Dark clouds in the sky had made the day most humid.
But kind of a cold feeling (for me alone) I felt in the
air that day. The sky was getting quite golden, too.*

*The tall palm trees were ruffling and flowery rose
trees were waggling—the sun was travelling to sink.*

*'Leave off worrying thoughts and come back to the
present, yaar,' said she.*

'But—'

*'Life is made of ifs and buts. So, keep that but aside,'
she neared and neatly sat beside me.*

'Huh!' muttered I.

She asked soberly, 'See, do you like my dress?'

'Expensive, indeed!' I opined.

'Develop an eye to see beauty!'

'Well, is it enough?'

'Come out of this dark cavern of worries! Life is precious! Live it full!' she advocated.

'But, what one can do when a thick line of poverty is inscribed on one's palm?' I revolted.

       Silence spread over there for a few minutes.

'Silly word!' she bounced on.

'Pet fate for a creature like me!' I

'Sad thinking always leads us to a sad destination.'

'That's why I'm destined to fight?'

'Gnawing of vitals; troubles much!'

'Representatively, I'm Doubting Thomas!'

'Clean your mind and come forward!'

'I've to achieve my goal.'

'Surely, you will!'

'By wasting time like this?'

'Soon time will disclose how far it's the waste of time!'

'Have you seen ever the king of doubts like me?'

'Yeh, the one who sat beside me!' and she smiled sensuously.

       A gentle puff of a warm (cold)
       breeze scattered her locks.
It beautified her face and made her cheeks more rosy.
       Sylphs and nymphs would save her beauty!
       And in the heart of my heart I
       longed for her to be my wife.

A traveller of an impossible path!
She might have sorted out those
dreamy emotions from my eyes!
Drawing a fresh breath, I glanced round.
Everything was quiet around.

'Sarita, why are we brought in here?' I asked her.
'For passing time!' she exclaimed punning on words.
'Please, break the ice!' I requested.
'That's the point I wanted to discuss in such a tranquil place!' she adoringly elucidated.
'A slight doubt hinders into my mind, if it is?' I muttered glancing around.
'King of doubts are you!' she laughed.
'I'm a laughing stock, indeed!'
'Needless to say!'
'Poor possesses prowess to prune ptomaine in poverty; thus poor can't be perplexed!'
'Excellent! Simply beautiful!'

Her praise for me was then interrupted
by the ring of her smartphone.

She walked away a few steps from me. Might be an urgent, important call? Then, she got herself busy in attending a call. Every throb of my heart was sounding a danger?

Far away lightning fluttered.
And Sarita was busy on her phone!
There appeared on my lips a gazal
of Sahir Ludhiyanwi.

Rang aur nasle—jat aur mazahab
Jo bhi ho aadmi se kamtar hai.
Jo bhi ho aadmi se kamtar hai.
Is haquikat ko tum bhi meri tarah
Maan jao to koi baat bane.

I thought I was soaring high in the sky
like a skylark singing a song of love!
Heaven knew I was far away from my cares, worries,
duties! That was an exalted, ecstatic moment, I hated
the silly world of pathos and cares. Had I ever thought
of a belle enamoured of a poor, poor boy like me!
She came back and sat down by me.
'Oh, my father is so careful a
man that he doesn't want
to keep his daughter away from his eyes!' she said.
'There is a near one for whom the main thing in life is
some attraction of the soul—that's called a father!'
Suddenly, a dreadful thought flashed through
my mind and struck upon my taut nerves.
I closed my eyes and took a deep breath.
Like a great lonely ram, I stalked
across my dreamland.
'When I consider life seriously, I find it is a cheat as
Jon Dryden thought it!' I opened a talk.
'What do you mean?' Sarita asked.
'I mean this life is a cheat,' I said.
'Man is life or life is man?'
'Difficult question, indeed!'

'What I mean who is cheat, man or life?' Sarita looked deeply into my eyes.

Sarita was the sort of girl I fancied.
I liked girls to be good-heighted, black-eyed, long black-haired, fair-complexioned, and full-breasted.
And she was the dream girl I dreamt.
I thought of her quite a lot.
But it would be funny if one of the poor souls like me used to being liked by girl like Sarita.
Prantik, my classmate at campus, said that it was her first lover a girl loved.
I laughed to myself for imagining I am being loved by Sarita.

'I say it is entirely true to have a nice talk today,' Sarita said.

'You brought in me here for, so why not?' I replied energetically.

'I'm afraid you will think my words wrong?' she blushed and hesitated.

'What made you think so?'

'Because of your traditional attitude.'

'Who said I'm traditional in my attitude?'

'You always think on the same line.'

'Better you say I'm conventional?'

'But we're the birds of modern time; so we must think progressively.'

'I confess that my trait of thinking is serious, but it's progressive too.'

My eyes followed her gesture.
She looked at me with amorous eyes.

Her look dashed me to thinking of too bold-
I like to take her in my arms, like to kiss those
bold and black eyes of hers, like
to sing a song for her -
silly thought, silly dream.
Why did she flash a look of her
beautiful black eyes at me?

'May I ask you one question?' she said.

'Of course, you may ask.'

'What's your idea of a life partner?'

'You mean a wife?'

'Of course!'

'It's sad that poor is not a chooser.'

'Poor, poor, poor! Why do you sing a ballad of this word?'

'Because poverty is the best ballad written by that almighty!'

'But in your case, I love this poverty!'

'It's simple to say this but—'I stammered.

'Difficult to bear, right?' she completed.

'Sarita, you don't go on this line. I pray the best ever life for you!' I said and bent my neck downward.

'The best ever life is my choice. And my choice is you.'

'My god!' I was caught by sheer surprise.

'Ajay, I love you very much. I like not only your personality but you heart. I see my safe future in you.'

I thought myself a little a man without temperament.
I didn't conceive any idea that something strange and
almost shocking had been darting in Sarita's mind.

Sarita turned to me and, taking my hand into hers, said
quite dreamily, 'Would you please give me a place into
your heart? See me as your wife?'
I felt a terrible shock of recognition in her.
But how could the two ends meet?
Sarita loved me.
But I straightly refused her proposal.
In the heart of my heart I sincerely didn't want to
make her a captive of poverty-loaded suffering.
Thereafter I made a bargain with my seriousness,
my composure, my loneliness, and my poverty.

LOVE THY NAME IS SUFFERANCE.
LOVE PROVES A SEISMIC OCCURRENCE.
LOVE THY NAME IS DISSEVERANCE.
LOVE ALLUS TEACHES FORBEARANCE.

For a moment, I thought myself a triumphant trooper!
My performance in the interview was satisfactory.
BUT
I started awaiting my recall anxiously.

WAITING FOR RESULT WAITING FOR RESULT
CONFUSION CONFUSION CONFUSION

October rainy evening was getting dark.
Gently my mind entered into the cavern of cares.

—hate—hate—hate—your son—father—scold severely—your son—mother—absurd son— mad son—your only son—failed—failed—didn't perform—rituals—didn't obey—customs—life— death—death—life—what's there—man's life— here—*i* came—wasted time—doubtful end—doubtful result—rude—unkind—negligent—culprit—your only son—is culprit—cruel—it won't—come back—that's final—unavoidable—father—pity me—father pity— me—mercy—mercy—mercy—save me—mother— save me—maya—save me—pity—mercy—mercy—

Followed by a big thunder, there came a recall for me.
My heart throbbed.
With a palpitating heart, I entered
the principal's cabin.
In the centre chair, the president was seated.
The secretary, hurriedly, came in and
sat in the left side corner chair.
All other chairs were vacant.

THE PRESIDENT THE SECRETARY
RESULT RESULT RESULT

There I observed a little change in that atmosphere.
With firm determination, I sat in
the chair on their asking.

'Well, we liked your performance,' the secretary opined.
'Thank you, sir!' I replied.

'You're still jobless, you know. If you're given a chance here in our college, what will you do for this college?' the secretary asked obliquely.

'Sir, I will, with humble measure of my capacity, put in my sincere efforts to serve this college as I always think education as a noble cause,' I tried to justify to his question.

'We want your sincere efforts, undoubtedly. There is no question about it, but we expect something more from you,' the secretary said in a silent tone.

His words paved a way of doubt in my mind.

The president was observing me very minutely.

'What do you expect from me, sir?' I asked clearly.

'See, for college development, we need money; a lot has to do for college. Development of the college is lagging behind due to short of money. So, looking at this point; I ask you—how much can you contribute—for the college development, really?' the secretary cleared my doubt.

The president smiled to himself and slightly
a candid look dazzled into his eyes.

CLEAR CLEAR CLEAR

I remained quiet for a minute.
The next moment, there rose a revolting spirit
in me and very confidently, I began to speak.
'Sir, let me beg your pardon first before speaking my words. Sir, I have been travelling and travelling—searching and searching—performing—presenting

myself to such interviews for the last six years. I have spent six valuable years of my life in search of a job. I possess all requisite qualifications. I stood second merit in my M A examination. Cleared NET and SET. But I don't have a job. I put in six years' strenuous struggle. I need a job, badly.'

The secretary instructed something to the peon, who stood at the door of the cabin.

The president peered at me.

'That all we know. You're a qualified and brilliant boy. We need you. But my question is, how much you can contribute?' the secretary repeated his words and ordered the peon to serve water.

I thought, that was the right moment for clearing the matter of contribution.

But I grew eager to know the actual amount of contribution from their tongues.

'Sir,' out of my curiosity, I asked, 'exactly how much do you expect from me?'

'It's known to us that you're not in a condition to contribute as per our expectation. Everything is growing in the market day by day. And what other college managements demand, we've nothing to do with that. But if the candidate is not ready to accept an adjustment my utterance is meaningless,' the secretary said.

MUCH EXPECTED MUCH EXPECTED

At the mention of the secretary's words, we (*the president and I*) stared at one another open-eyed.

I thought over it for a while.

That was a terrific situation!

The words pierced my ears.
I was recoiled in fear.
At that moment I reviewed the whole sad,
pathetic sequence of events in my life.
Then I made myself ready to take care
never to hear such words thereafter.

'Sir, your suggestion,' I started strongly, 'is all right. But I'm a penniless boy. Even a penny is a dream for me; really a dream! At this moment I have only twenty-seven rupees in my pocket clearly hundred rupees short of my return bus ticket. I'm sorry. I can't go along this way. That's my confirmation.'

I completed my words in a single breath.

'Think over it. It's a chance. Service isn't sold out in market?' the secretary said.

Both of them tried to read my face.

'Wrong, sir. Wrong words you're speaking?' I revolted.

The president stared at me.

A rude reactionary look of the secretary
made me more aggressive.
But, I had made up my mind to
revolt against such practices.
The president and the secretary
looked at one another wilfully.

'What's wrong; what's right; we know it better. You aren't here to teach us—are you?' the secretary raised his voice. But the president smiled secretly.

'It's not at all the question of teaching, sir. But, you used the words: service isn't sold out in market. That's why I revolted. Isn't it a market when the candidate is asked to accept an adjustment in this form? Tell me sir, isn't it a market?' I flung my hesitation.

'We're ready to give you a chance. That's why a direct method. Think over it,' the president opened his mouth. But his eyes were smashing a kind of suspicious emotion, rather difficult to gaze!

'No, sir. I am unable to agree your words. I'm a poor boy,' said I firmly.

'So, what will you do with your qualifications? You must have to do an adjustment if you want service. After all, we offer you a chance of adjustment,' the secretary spoke again.

The peon brought two *bislery* bottles
and served water to them.

Although I was very thirsty, I dared not ask for water. 'Sir, don't misunderstand me,' I began, 'what I'm going to speak. *If you can't stand the heat; get out of the kitchen.* It's Harry S Truman's quote. So, frankly speaking sir, I can't take the pressure of this adjustment, so it will be better to remove myself from this situation,' said I.

The president, then, looked
intentionally at the secretary.

The secretary shrugged his shoulders.

'You're not an adjustable boy, I say. So, we can't help you,' the secretary hushed.

'Right, sir. I'm not an adjustable boy. You may call it my arrogance or attitude. But there is no one reason for my inability to accept your condition. Instead, I bear some of my own principles. I'm astutely determined not to accept any demand of service if it is conditional—mean such kind of adjustment. If I do this, it will be a criminalisation of my principles. I'm not a vulnerable soul to singing a soliloquy *to die or not to die* and it's not at all the agonising question for me. The crux of this matter is that the choice should be of the candidate appearing for interview or his personal decision. It's his legitimate right. In my opinion, there should be no dilly-dallying in practicing such adjustment. So, I won't accept your proposal. I will go without service, will do any job or work, but never kill my principles and for this arrogance you may call me a rude or haughty, or ill-bred stupid boy.' I demonstrated my views strongly.

The president remained quiet in his chair.

The secretary's eyes flared up with surprise.

It was time for my exit from there.

'What's your father?' the president moved his question, when I was about to make an exit from there.

At once my father's virtuous face
appeared into my eyes.
And my legs touched the earth.
My heart sank into my boots; a
strange fear caught me a whole.
My eyelids flapped with tears.
Controlling my emotion, I turned back
and stood bending my neck.

'My father was a farmer, sir,' I said sadly.

'So, he is no more?' the president asked.

'Yes, he is dead. And the truth is that, my father died of severe heart-attack last night without giving any

alarming call. And leaving my father's corpse there at home without attending his funeral obsequies, his only son came here for interview only for keeping family's bread and butter. Sir, my hard-working father is no more. This only son proved himself—prodigal—better you call me a killer—killer of father,' I summed up.

Tears in my eyes barricaded my words.
Then quickly I made my exit from the cabin.
Was I a sourpuss?
Outside it was getting dark.
Like a debt-crippled client, I reached
sadly to the classroom.
Suddenly, I felt very weak and weary.
The tears welled up to my eyes.
I was late.
I must have to get a quick move on.
My legs trembled a little as I stood at the door.
Dewkar, Dongre, and that girl were waiting outside.
Mahadeo looked at me and brought
a glass of water for me.
I drank water and thanked him.
He smiled and said, 'Good luck, *beta*!'
'Good luck!' But what for? Everything was over.
I had declined an opportunity and
Mahadeo said, 'Good luck?'
Bafflement ascended on me.
My father's dead body dazzled my eyes.
Looking at the mild drizzle, I quickly
stepped forward on my way back.

But to my surprise, I was called back by the principal.

SUSPENSE SUSPENSE SUSPENSE
DOUBT DOUBT DOUBT

As I reached the principal's cabin, I
had seen Sarita coming out of it.
'Hearty congratulations! Meet the president.
Waiting you outside,' said she joyously.
Sarita's words *Hearty Congratulations* stunned my
ears and in a frenzy of ecstatic joy forgot to thank her.

I entered the cabin with mixed emotions.
The principal asked me to sit in the chair.

'Okay. Your test is over. Take those words of mine
as examiner's words. You're selected by the selection
committee. You will receive your appointment order
by post or if you wish you can collect it from the office
after a week. We hope your joining immediately, but
keep your word to put in your best efforts to serve the
noble cause of education—as you said. In fact, we want
a boy like you who can come up with a kind of daring
and commitment as shown by you. I pray for your
father. Don't bother and discharge your duties in the
college with full determination. Give me the results,'
the president said thoughtfully.

Tremendous joy brightened my face.
I expressed my sincere thanks to the
president and the secretary.

Then I met the members of the selection
committee and thanked them.
And I made my exit with quite a mixed emotion.
At the door of the classroom,
Sarita was waiting for me.
I couldn't meet my eyes with hers for a while.
'Quite a good performance you have
delivered. Join immediately,' Sarita said.
It was after a long period that her sweet
words resonated into my ears.
Words defeated me.
I couldn't utter even a word that moment.
A fragrance of plentiful roses had
lodged into her elegant smile.
Four eyes conversed with each other.
Lips uttered the past; asked us both how to depart.
When I departed from there, I saw a thin
flow of tears rolling down her eyes.

No sooner did I cross the porch than Mahadeo's words arrested my ears. At once Mahadeo came near and patted me back lovingly, congratulated me heartily and put two notes on my hand.

'Two thousand rupees!' I exclaimed.

'Keep it for your travel. Accept my little help. I know all about your condition,' he said and went back quickly.

Looking up at the dark sky, I uttered:
O lord, munificence is still alive!

But, how could I repair the loss I had met in life.
May I bring back my father to life?

May I see my father again?
Anna, I succeeded to keep our bread
and butter—I moaned.

Filled with a drastic fear and mother's care,
I walked on the way to the bus station.
Anna's last words reverberated into my ears: My dear son, I'm taking my exit from this world -- dying a natural death—of an untreated disease—called heart attack—a cause bestowed upon me by Heaven. I'm proud, I served my land with humble measure of my capacity and ability as a farmer. Many of my fellow farmers have accepted death untimely—committing suicide—taking it as a final path of freedom from—precious life. Death is a leveller, my son. Don't consider my death, in any way, a suicide—farmer's suicide. Remember, don't take life as the primrose path—life is all challenge till one kicks the bucket. Go along your way—honestly—

Printed in the United States
By Bookmasters